PETRIFICATION
and other short stories

REGGIE DAVID

Brilliant Books Literary
137 Forest Park Lane Thomasville
North Carolina 27360 USA

Contents

You've Heard about Beelzebub the Demon; Now Meet Beelzebub the Hero

Reeves Filburn was drinking his gin Milby, with wife Claire, sporting his double tweed Italian flax knit three-piece dinner jacket ensemble when he stepped through a doorway and came upon Beelzebub the demon.

Reeves stammered, "Er, hello, Beel, ole fellow, we hadn't expected you at the Rothchild's. They always throw a party of this sort at this time of year."

He glanced at Claire, who wore the appropriate greeting smile. Reeves's number one peeve was to stammer in public, and he bit back on his anguish for having made such a callous first impression. The fact hovering in the minds of both him and his wife was that the demon at any instant could kill them both.

Beelzebub stood six feet four inches at four hundred pounds in his brown leather loin strap equipped with side satchel full of confusion powder and a cheap propeller instrument he used for blowing it in peoples' faces. The powder was composed of some god-awful narcotic he'd ripped off from a kid at a carnival several time zones before. His own mischievous ingredients completed the concoction. The propeller instrument also had been taken from the cherry cotton candy–mouthed, fat kid behind a building with a hard right fist into the kid's pudgy jaw. Under an elongated pause in this room otherwise empty save the three, Reeves stammered a second time to his own disgust but then recovered himself emphatically.

"Um, the London bombing was his feet stomping!"

Reeves said this with a "hi-ho" cheers motion of his drink. He then downed the rest of it. His wife, Claire, did the same and giggled appropriately, actually saying the words "hi-ho" while raising her glass. They then looked at each other intently. All they could do to hide their shock and fear of being killed was continue with an act of being civil to the demon, as if he were another guest at the party.

Beelzebub, you could say, was not in his top form. The reality of being a demon such as he was, was that occasionally there were times like this—when, for lack of being able to find evil to commit, he would wander about from one obscure setting to another aimlessly, ending up in awkward situations around people he had no interest in whatsoever. He had just spent days traveling with a rock band in a bus on tour, acting as a representative with their recording label and engaging in binge drug consumption of just about every kind of substance known and combinations thereof. He had been back and forth from the concerts to red-light districts to carnivals—finding people, scoring drugs, and bringing them back to the band then partying with mass consumption backstage and on the road. He lost interest in them and transported out through cities and over country and ocean, not caring where he would materialize, in a random direction, to appear here.

Beelzebub had the face of a decaying bull with glazed eyes, black-and-white feathers, lizard-like black claws for hands, and huge black rat's paws for feet. He didn't know where he was or how he got here, but he was becoming slightly aware there were two people standing next to him and he could kill them. His head immediately changed into that of a giant mynah bird, and he let out a beastly cackle, "A-hah!" His feet changed into bovine hoofs and started stomping to no beat. His head began to bow and thrust upward, and his arms began a sweeping motion that made circles and stopped in front, like putting eggs in a basket, as his whole body turned to face his two victims.

Reeves said, "Well, I believe this is a dance of some sort," and began attempting to repeat step by step the nonrhythm of the hoofs colliding with the wood floor in the wooden room, as Claire joined him. It was a dance. It was Beelzebub's patented Death Dance, and he was about to rip these two complete idiots to shreds. He had gone quickly from being in a sedated daze to the insane ecstasy of his ritualistic Death Dance, which he always performed when killing. The beak of his face hung open with malice as his body gyrated at the torso. He grew to nine hundred pounds, and his face became that of a baboon with stiff, long outward jackal ears. His laugh echoed against the wooden walls a loud, shrill baboon scream. He looked at the two hopping little idiots and started developing a full circular motion with the left arm while at the end of it metamorphosed a solid, high-carbon metal bludgeoning wrist simply cubic in shape to cleave the first idiot through the brain. The woman he would kill by ripping her throat out with the right claw. He pitied them, their ridiculous curiosity drawn to his feet and trying to imitate his clomping. Their lives were nothing more than impetuous imitation and conformity to others. They were better off dead. The demon could picture times of high stress in their lives when matters of finance forced them to consider all alternatives and left them praying and confused. They were born confused. They should also die that way.

The demon reached for the propeller with the right arm, dipped it into the powder and thrust it into the man's face, squeezing the two gear sticks together. It blew white powder into Reeves's face. He did the same for the woman while maintaining the swinging bludgeon arm and hoof stomp. The two began to waiver with consternation on the brow. Reeves stammered for a third time because of the powder in his face, but his mood changed.

Blinking, he said, "Beel, ole lad, I, I don't believe I can keep step with you. Well, well, that's it. I'm confused!"

Reeves looked up in the demon's face only inches away from his, its eyes huge and malevolent. Reeves chuckled a bit, "H-hah," and he became rather giddy. Claire giggled. Beelzebub's bludgeoning arm swung to a standstill above Reeves's head. Reeves's and Claire's laissez-faire mannerism threw Beelzebub off guard.

The confusion powder had backfired. It was supposed to make them baffled and apprehensive. With Beelzebub, it was the little things. He could not take seriously any homicidal action upon them with them behaving so silly. His mood immediately changed into a self-absorbed manic depression very common for him. This was Beelzebub's other side in which he frequently remained emotionally distraught and withdrawn.

When this mood hit him, he became weakened, clumsy, and harmless as a mouse. He began to transform. The swinging bludgeon arm became a marshmallow texture that wouldn't cleave open an eggshell at certain angles. The claw hand with cheap propeller instrument turned into a paper machete hollow texture and broke off.

Claire glanced at it broken on the floor and said, "Oh, dear," with a fanciful look of viewing something nasty. The demon was shrinking rapidly down to 120 pounds, and his head became that of a gray housecat.

Reeves chuckled outright, "He's ridiculous, isn't he?"

Beel's feathers had turned from shiny black and white to embarrassing red and white. Reeves and wife began to walk backward through the door they came, trying not to be noticed. Seeing the demon reduced to this state even drew a feeling of pity from Reeves.

"So good to have met your acquaintance, sir," he remarked, and they both exited.

Beel had a hard time balancing when he was like this, even though his feet changed to monkeyish pink bipedals. He lost another thirty pounds down to ninety and collapsed on a couch. He now had the head of a rhesus monkey with a bird's beak, a small curly tongue sticking out to one side and childish doll eyes. There was a door at the other end of the room on the same wall opposite the couch. Some loud people came through it holding drinks—jewelry and dresses cladding the women, of course.

One black-haired woman peered forward to Beel and waved, "Oh, hi," as other voices said, "Nothing in here."

The convergence walked the distance to the door Reeves had come through and exited. Beelzebub drowned in his own self-pity now with flies buzzing about his head. He said in a squeamish little child's voice coming out of his beak…

Beelzebub

Beelzebub

Beelzebub…bub…bub…bub

Meet the Parkers

There walked the Parkers—the offspring Tony, middle child girl Angie, and last but not least, Mike. All in their thirties and each involved with their own nuclear kin, they shared an anonymous day of shopping with their father, Frank, and mother, Christine. Through the urban concrete structures all offering purchasables for competitive prices, they walked, daughters of the American Revolution and white Anglo-Saxon protestant to the core, in tune with the crawling hum of civilians crowding the downtown shopping area the day after the Fourth of July.

As they left Maxie's designer department store, their conversation meandered as always, chokingly discreet and polarized from anything resembling controversy. Through the revolving glass doors, they all looked up simultaneously to gaze at the huge and ominous billboard, which took much of the space of the corner building at an elevated height across the intersection. It was stuck in the middle of a commercial spiel. Instead of reading, "Don't think, don't eat, don't speak, just drink Diet..." it was stuck on the words "Don't speak." The parkers stopped all in their tracks and stared at the words then shuffled on. They did not open their mouths at all for the time after, going into Placard's Bounty. They silently viewed items, purchased a few, and left the store with a few more bags to carry.

Outside the automatic doors, the Parkers metamorphosed into two-dimensional, life-size, expressionless cardboard replicas of themselves and levitated slowly above ground, as a crowd gathered in an audience like circle around them.

Tony Parker blurted out in a monotone, amplified, and rather tiny, static voice, "Every day I have to introduce myself as a suppressed magnate rather than the billionaire mogul, which I dream of being. There shall come a day in which I overcome. I shall overcome. I shall overcome. I shall overcome some day. Deep in my heart, I do believe that I shall overcome some day…"

The crowd slightly clapped, and a dim "whooo" was heard. As the words had come out of his mouth, the cardboard lips had simply opened and closed, not even in good timing with the phonic sound of his voice. The next vocal was Mike Parker.

"I understand the injustices brought forth by a new nation, indivisible, with infractions for all to consume."

Then spoke Angie Parker, with the same monotone, tiny, amplified voice not sounding in sync with the up-an-down motion of the cardboard lips, "My lipstick's pastel pink and my lingerie pink lace with thong panties. I'm a hot mama on the move. You better run fast to catch me. Fashion, dig it on the left. Fashion, see it on the right. Fashion. Fashion. Yeah, yeah, yeah."

Then spoke out the father Frank Parker…"It was that darn mechanic who wouldn't fix the car. On that day I left my family stranded at the mall. A responsible father I am. Say it loud, say it proud, a happy dad I am."

Then Christine Parker, "My children grew up to be or not to be, that was their condition. You see them standing healthy and fine. The lesson is, you can't change a person unless they love you, then it is a change for the better. Oh, yeah! Gimme a whoooooiee!"

The crowd imitated her, "Whoooooiee!"

A young African American man with a boom box jumped back slightly with a surprised expression in his eyes and his mouth forming an *O* shape when the device he was holding took on a life of its own and ignited three-quarter volume with a heavy drum and symbol dance beat. He let it do its thing. It was obviously part of this weird show. The cardboard Parkers, still levitating above the crowd where they could be viewed by all, started moving their feet and legs slightly to the beat. Their bodies were movable at the joints sort of like plastic skeletons are joined and jointed. Frank Parker spoke out like a rapper in the same monotone, tiny, amplified voice,

> If you came to jive
> Just come alive
> Look all around
> And get on down

His cardboard form moved back among the others, and they formed a V-shape with Mike in front, Tony and Angie, and then Frank and Christine in the back. They started moving in a choreographed number, kicking out their legs and "worming" the arms, shoulders, necks, and heads with their fingers interlocked. The crowd was clapping in time, and some were picking up their feet and stomping slightly.

Tony moved to the front of the V-formation and rapped,

> This conclusion is a delusion
> The results of a higher education The results of
> medication
> The results evade you The method aids you
> The pressure point turns blue

He did a very strident but skillful twisting and kicking dance move and got back in the V-formation behind Mike. Just then, a man in the crowd came out with a microphone, and his voice could be heard over another speaker somewhere…

"Oh, yeah! Tony Parker does the robot spin! You've seen it on Soul Train." Christine moved to the front of the V-formation and rapped her lyric,

> Now I'm the mama of the bunch
> I've got a good suspicious hunch
> I make 'em all dinner and lunch
> So they can have that food to munch

She moved to the back of the V-formation as the dancing Parkers all clapped and rotated, their eyes as usual expressionless and fixated forward. The man with the microphone said, "Oh, yeah! Mama Parker, give her a hand," and the crowd appropriately clapped and "whooood." Mike's turn to rap came up, but instead he became abstract…

"Does the night fold, or is it latticework of woven silk binding? Calliopes are included in the subset of cornucopias, chaise lounges, foyers, gazebos, and belfries."

Then Tony broke in, "In the aftermath of yesterday consternation ceases the decrepit ending forthrightly as mass is held, such deafening sonic boom volume."

The Slender Cow/Horse

The slender cow/horse woke up early in the morning to the joyous sound of birds in its bed of hay. It got up and started walking the path to the pea/berry patch. Habitually, it ate the pea/berries continuing in a chewing motion for a length of time, of course avoiding the thorns. Along came the friendly bull/dog. He was too short to reach the pea/berries. The friendly bull/dog, jealous of the slender cow's/horse's ability to eat the pea/berries made this action. It jumped up to the mouth of the slender cow/horse and tried to imitate the eating action, bumping the opening and closing mouth of the slender cow/horse. The slender cow/horse buckled slightly and whinnied/mooed, as it was licking its lips. The slender cow/horse was licking so much! The friendly bull/dog then jumped a few more times, meeting the opposing mouth and then became passive and walked away. In the history of both animals at this area, this exchange had taken place with exactly the same rhythm exactly twenty-one times.

After eating, the slender cow/horse continued down the path. It walked pace after pace in the noonday sun, licking its lips and teeth and thinking of how good the purple pea/berries always tasted. It found the familiar-looking glass/pond. With vanity, it gazed at its reflection in the looking glass/pond, as the water sat still in the windless noonday air.

Just then, the dangerous mudpuppy sprang out of the water and clasped the slender cow/horse by the throat. With a ferocious back-and-forth gnashing of its head, it tore at the slender cow's/horse's neck and found the jugular artery. As the slender cow/horse reared on its hind legs in horror and anguish, its front legs treaded air. The dangerous mudpuppy made one tremendous pull, and the entire bloodstream of the slender cow/horse drained as its body fell headfirst into the water in a macabre, slo-mo, soundless scene.

The pond turned a miraculously sickening puke-red with coagulants floating in it, expanding outward in a flower-like shape toward the edges.

Two Lingering Questions

1) The name for the coagulation in the looking glass/pond, and

2) The whereabouts of the dangerous mudpuppy

The Subliminal Voice of Liberty

I was on vacation in Jamaica, wandering through shanty town, meandering at the tables of beads and necklaces offered. At the end of a long street was a house with front open and writings laid out on a blanket that looked to be occult-oriented. There was a heavy smell of marijuana from inside the house. A black man came out with dreadlocks and a T-shirt that had the saying with a marijuana leaf emblem "Legalize It."

He said to me, "You one tourist, man? Go 'head and sit down right dar in 'at chair. I got one narrative for you. This is 'The Subliminal Voice of Liberty' by Freddy Vincent."

He looked at some papers in his hand and started reading,

Beckon the bats revolving around
Belfry cats afire as they hit the ground Action
from impact pumped up afoot Authority
explodes, gone evil, kaput

The acrid air is sweet sensation 'Tis the liberation
of the nation Faggots afire! Seen dead and gone
Jelicho twilight, beaten at dawn

The subliminal voice I've heard in my mind
Speaks future tense, leaving the past behind If
liberty ye seek, then truth you will find
O'er land and sea down streets paved and lined

Mine eyes have seen what is sure to come
A new gleaming carcass without purr or hum
Eclipsed is a flag dyed red, white, and green An
era, an area for King Captain Mean

The civil, the political, divided king three The
forth made command by killing King B Next in
command, how to kill King A
And bring about our final new day

As the three kings burned in prayin' pain The
city in chaos, run safe or be slain!
Bullets pop-popping here, there, everywhere
And two angels gassed, screaming, "Who lit my
hair?"

The last lead trigger punk needing a theme Put
end to all mercy, his soul to redeem One angel
down, now needing the other Our security
system beats all Big Brother

Pow, then fall second angel bleeding and pure
Hail land, my green flag, reflection be sure Into
the pool jumped those who were agile
Lincoln's knowing gaze thought their lives were
fragile

Second flank of runners and those bearing arms
Joined forces seeing the signs and alarms
Took cover in tunnels, John Brown's body harms
Secure underground transport, then send back
to farms
Gaining control of whole mobile system

Ring finger of new army thrilled them and
kissed 'em Could then flow smooth to recruit
second city
Three factors: arms, might, and electricity

The fuel of force rages for or against us The
army of old is stalled on one big bus
Our new day dawns, our wise man demands
As one we take both with our feet and our hands

Occupied hoods come richer and new Must
bring back purity to kill the shrew What once
was ours we worked so hard for
Bought as if auctioned by beast and a whore

Oh! Excuse me if I was wrong Just listen now to
my rhyme song:

Oh, say, can you see by the dawn's early light
What now to soon day should always be night
Our system was smooth, our flag red, white,
and blue The last gleaming trickster passed
green on to you How cold you will be in our
black spider's web Perilous bored widow! Off
offspring which bled Widow can't kill male,
from broad bars and stripes Eternally anxious
yet airing her gripes
Gallant and holding the flame that amaze Can
melt and get lazy in two hateful days
Drop tablet, truth gone, hell raised in a phrase
Arm free, flame down, block burned in a blaze!

I stared at him for a while, his words hypnotizing me. I said nothing
as he looked distantly forward. He didn't seem to notice me anymore. I
started walking away. It had been hot August summer, the year of 2001.

Weeks later when the events of 9/11 hit, I thought of how reminiscent his anarchistic poem had been of the chaos in New York and Washington. I looked back down the dirt road avenue lined with crafts for tourists and the voices of people seemed so far off. There was no one at the man front of the house anymore. I had forgotten to pay him for his narrative but fancied that some things were too profound for money. I turned and was on my way.

Morbidity

The king stood with his men on horseback, a formidable army. In the dark sky at dawn were he and hundreds. His men whom he had lived and fought with now faced an equal opponent. They sat on horseback, estimating the opposing force from across the valley, feeling the impending seriousness of what could be their last moments of life. It was the time before they charged. Just then a horrendous cavalry appeared, charging over a near mountainside to join the army in the valley. It was a surprise attack. With the combined forces, the king and his men would be massacred.

He spoke out, "The time is nigh, and it is time to die. In the end, we were all men. Our times were had, our suns settin' free, our cause was true, followed our beliefs, we. Now face an inevitable end, us."

As the knights in armor clashed, the sound of swords piercing flesh, the sound of throats crying then slashed silent, the sound of horses hoofs stomping, the sound of horses whinnying and crying, the sound of men roaring in horror, and the sound of death growls filled the air. His men surrounded the king in a circle to protect him, but soldier after soldier was outnumbered and killed. The king's horse spun in frenzied circles as he waved his sword above his head and screamed aloud, witnessing the fall of his army in an outpouring of spraying blood and surrounded by the sound of MORBIDITY.

You are walking through the jungle with an M-16 rifle sweating slightly in fatigues and combat boots. You hear bird sounds and the wind slightly shaking the trees. In a clearing, you see the shocking image of a soldier who disappeared from your platoon. He is suffering from a special type of torture in which he is bound by the feet and hands, fully stretching the arms, legs and whole body out with tight force. Cord tied around the wrists and ankles wraps around bamboo stakes pounded firmly into the ground, suspending the body about a foot above the floor of the jungle. With this torture method, the cartilage at all the joints in the arms, legs, and vertebrae of the backbone slowly stretches apart and causes an excruciatingly painful, slow death.

You toss your weapon onto the ground and reach for your comrade's head, hanging loose backward.

Raising it up, his eyes are wide open with a look of hazy, wild bewilderment and his mouth jarred open as he breathes in shallow gasps.

He says, "Hu, hu, help me."

You reach for your knife in its holster on your belt to cut at the cord of one of the wrists. Just as you begin cutting, you hear movement in the bushes through the clearing. It is the enemy. You have no time to reach for your weapon just as you see a rifle held at you with arms holding and a determined face looking down the sights. With one shot fired out, you are pierced through the head, and your body falls lifeless directly onto your tortured comrade. The weight of you hitting him causes a severe shock of pain for him, making much worse the stretching force on his body.

He screams in pain, "Aaaughgh"

The enemy soldiers check the area for others, aiming their weapons forward and panning from side to side. They look down at the tied, tortured one screaming and gasping with the dead one shot in the head strewn lifeless across the chest. They move on through the trees with an arm motion and command from the leader, the last one gazing back at the sight of the two.

The last dying gasps of the tied soldier emerge from the wide-open mouth as his head hangs back. The scene is quiet with the steady sound of birds and trees rattling from a slight breeze. Blood drips from the bullet hole in the eye socket of the shot soldier, in a steady stream down his forehead and onto the ground, gathering in a small puddle. The bodies will remain there and begin decaying, to be found months ahead with insects and worms having eaten the flesh in a moribund mass.

The stark reality of war.

The shocking horror of death. The essence of MORBIDITY

There is a presence. It hovers in a bleak, pale hallway of a hospital ward. It moves slowly down the hall and comes upon a doorway. Turning in to the room, there are several doctors in white jackets quietly consulting each other, one holding a chart. They stand around a bed with the body of a woman who has been in a coma from car accident for months. The heart rate monitor slowly beeps. An IV hangs from its rung with tubing plugged into one arm under a bandage. A respirator steadily breaths air into the mouth and nose covered with a mask. The body has deteriorated down to an emaciated skeleton. It will never recover consciousness but only remain in its solitary stasis worse than death.

The doctors move away, and the one holding the chart hangs it on the front of the bed. They walk out of the room turning the light off. The presence looms over the body for a great amount of time as it lies still in the darkness, never to move a single muscle again. The presence slowly withdraws from the bed, toward the doorway. Down the hall it hovers steadily past several rooms. The end of the hall is a plain white wall with no window and nothing such as a bulletin board, the doorway to the last room being at the side. The presence enters the room.

It has only one bed. On it lays an abomination of a human being. The victim of a land mine explosion, its legs were blown off at the pelvis and arms at the shoulders. Its face was blown off, removing all the skin with lower jaw, tongue, and upper teeth, and leaving only a hole at the throat. The eyes were blown out of the sockets and the nose gone, leaving only an exposed nasal passage to breathe through. Also, the ears were blown off and the eardrums ruptured. It suffered a great near-fatal trauma, leaving it without sense of sight, sound, smell, or taste.

With what little body left, it can only feel without hands the sheets covering it. Fed through a tube at the throat hole, it only exists in an extremely limited sense, moving the head slightly from side to side in a constant state of bewilderment and blindness. A cover hides its hideous exposed skull. It isn't even sure if it is alive at all. It only remains in a continuing mutilated dimension.

It is the embodiment of MORBIDITY.

You are a police officer. A rookie. You are becoming acquainted with a range of experiences and beginning to form a schema of what to expect during a typical night of patrol. The radio blurts out a call to your car in the area to respond, and your partner accelerates the vehicle. A disturbance in an abandoned building. You arrive at the scene. It is a dark, decrepit building looming in the night sky. There are no lights at all. No electricity. Condemned notices are posted on doors and the fence surrounding it. Sections of the fence have been torn down. There are complaints of people having been seen trespassing here. Your partner and you walk the perimeter, looking for an open door. You find a doorway with the large wooden door broken into pieces and hanging from its hinges. You shine your flashlights into the darkness of the hallway littered with newspapers and other trash. You walk up a staircase to the second floor and down another hall. You hear the sound of whispering and voices emanating from behind one of the doors. You enter the large room with readiness and apprehension.

It is a shooting gallery. Scattered over the floor are a number of junkies, some shaking and rocking back and forth, some warming their hands by candles, some in the act of injecting themselves with a syringe and some asleep with newspapers covering their heads. One of them yells, "It's the cops!" and there is some commotion as one or two of them runs out of the room by connecting doorways. Your partner tells you, "Let him go," as he holds on to your forearm. Most of the junkies are too stoned or despondent to care about you shining the flashlight in their faces, if they are conscious at all. You make your way around the room cluttered with cardboard boxes and cheap stands being used for tables. At the back wall with windows is another short hallway into a small room. You are a police officer and should be desensitized, but you must brace yourself for the hideous scene you now find.

Entering the room, the flashlights beam onto a small walking form that creeps out of the darkness. It is a child. But it is not at all endearing. It has ripped clothing and tousled hair. It is emaciated. It is barefoot in this near-freezing cold. When it walks closer, you are repulsed by it and gasp in a lungful of air as your partner and you rear a step backward. You can see its chest move in and out as it breaths shallow breaths.

It speaks, "Mommy won't move. Why won't my mommy move?"

You pan the flashlight the breadth of the room. On the floor in the corner is a body lying still on its back with arms splayed out. You step closer to see. It is a woman with eyes wide open in a blank stare.

Dead. Mouth wide open in a final gasp. A needle hangs punctured into her arm, not having been removed before the hotshot-caused fatality. The child kneels by her shoulder and pushes at the rib cage, gently disturbing its dead mother, then places a hand on the hair and stares into its blank face. You don't know what to do. You can't pull the child back off its mother. You don't even want to touch the child at all. You know that you will have to take it by the arm and lead it away from the corpse, and it will scream and cry when you do so, but for now both your partner and you are mortified in a moment of realistic shock. The child is like a festering rat. It looks as if it has never been exposed to sunlight. You can't even tell what gender it is. It stands up and stares at you with wild eyes as gasps of breath form mist in front of its mouth. The expression on its face seems to say, "Well, what are you going to do?" And you still can't move. All you can do is stare back at its horrid form.

It is the visage of pestilence. It is the image of MORBIDITY.

You can't think. You have just woken and are trying to suppress the nightmares you just had. In the mind is a blurred vision of the globe, rotating and showing time zones. You're sure that its presence is that of an invasive foreign body. Problems are being ripped apart in your mind, leaving you senseless, helpless. Before solutions can be grasped, they are "reached out" to by gummy white fingers of writhing thin hands. Thoughts become words, and words become meaningless. Apocalypse, divorce us as we engage hierarchies of business venture in our coldest climactic interval. The time zones of the world are being glued to by the fingers and reversed and rearranged. The maps of earth's continents are diluted land masses completely unfamiliar. A grinding machine sound is heard as the distorted globe rotates in your mind, along with a throbbing hum so loud you think your head may burst.

Then silence. A scene with innocent, joyous children flashes into your mind with the sound of a *click* from a slide projector. Then another picture of children playing in a sunny field shows with another *click* sound, as children's laughter plays faintly in the background. It is like a frame-by-frame still movie. Scene after scene of children playing in a field is shown in black and white, slightly faded pictures—each one coming with a *click* sound. Then the last picture goes, leaving only blackness as the distant voices fade out. You notice that your eyes can't see anything other than what is inside your head. You become aware that you are completely disoriented. You have lost your sense of balance and sense of direction completely. You don't even know which way is forward and your in-head ocular sense is searching to reestablish a left and right. Then a surprise conscious pops up in a direction which you can't discern to be left, right, forward, backward, or even up or down. It looks to have emerged from between a plane where a panel cuts off from your ocular sense and reaches an indiscernible "wall," the outside limit of your in-head vision. It is hunched, humanoid, and shadowed. It seems to be in a costume of skin-tight black body suit, with a long tail, and it shows white gloved hands.

It sees you.

It is inside you.

It knows you can see it.

You don't want it to be there.

If you could reach out to it with your arms and grab it, you would tear it to pieces. It stands still with only a slight wavering of its arms hanging by its sides.

It quivers. It fears you.

It stares continuously back at you with its whitish pale face and the beady eyes of a cowardly criminal.

In a squeaky mouse voice, it speaks,

"I am MORBIDITY."

I will arrive. Within timelessness and illusiveness, there will not be a way out. I will come to you in your sleep in the form of the skeleton of death, knocking on your open door. I will offer you alternatives in your life to come—all of which lead down the same road of hopelessness to a dead end years ahead where you loathe your plain life and career and only dream of how things could have been different. You will come to me through tunnels, deepening, triangular riveted partitions segmenting air. Spiraling down into an abyss and one tunnel curving 'round. Through the first and out into a pit below bottomlessness, the second pounding unconscious against a brick wall. Both come together and arrive. I will stalk you every day as you try to run away from the inevitable conclusion of depression, obscurity, and death. From the center of earth I am harbored, from the dawn of time I existed, and from all depths and heights I surround you.

Again you awake. You realize with a shock of horror that you are stuck in a cycle where you keep waking up repeatedly. You can't be sure if you are awake. The next day is here. You wonder if it will be the same asphyxiating monotony as every day is. You hope not. The feet twitch. You may now come alive. Two doors open, and through them you may wander. You stand. The weight of self is stable. Inside is as always ill. In mind a vision of a noose. Walking down the hall in the same suit, giving the usual "hi-ho" and "good day," you see the same pale, lifeless, and paranoid people you do every day. At the door at the end of the hall, you pass through and find your body levitating in blue sky with clouds flying over. Looking down, your feet are touching nothing, and there is no land and only sky to be seen. You have become trapped within a bizarre three-dimensional movie, and your body is being controlled and led involuntarily through a freakish plot. Meaningless scenes are being changed and shown in the space surrounding you.

The next scene appears. Downhill you sled. Someone's childhood or your own, you think. For a moment, there is childish joy. Inertia carries you swiftly down through moist air. Children's voices are heard screaming playfully, and you are filled with the warmest sense of well-being. Suddenly, the scene dissipates with an electric snap. Off-whiteness flashes into a rectangular border; then suddenly it is checkerboard with huge white-and-black squares. You're body, having been shocked upright against it, is stuck nose to the white. Frustration, aggravation, and angst collapse into your middle ear. Your head explodes.

The black square drops back like a trick door. A huge cigarette protrudes out, piercing your abdomen, ripping guts out and cracking the vertebrae at the lumbar and below the rib cage. The guts fall to the floor with a sloshing sound. The floor is a plaster plastic with your feet cemented in. However, your upper body remains suspended above the lower, both partially petrified against an abstract plane. The plane intersects the floor. With a quaking sound of something like heavy machinery dropping into gear, it moves back. You are distanced from the checkerboard wall as a second loud machine sound occurs. The wall begins moving slowly sideways and gains speed. The distancing stops with a loud *clack* machine sound, and the wall speeds up into a blur with an accompanying humming and grinding sound. A static is created with air friction as the wall blends into a pulsating gray.

A loud popping sound occurs behind the plane. It is a solid, heavy metal strobe light. It begins to flash onto the wall, showing the shadow of your gutted and decapitated body. Then a movie flashes onto the wall, emanating from the strobe and showing a scene of trees swaying in the wind with several birds flying from tree to tree. The motion of the scene is slightly segmented and rather slo-mo. The sound of the birds chirping fluctuates in range like a tape slowing down and speeding up, from a wooden recorder at low to a flute at high. Another machine sound occurs, and your suspended body rotates ninety degrees then stops.

You are an actor.

You are a dismembered actor next to a sick screen on a mutated stage in front of a ghost audience following a mute script.

The name of the play is *MORBIDITY*.

Suddenly, the strobe disappears with a snap. The speeding wall fades quickly, leaving a blue sky scene with clouds, over and all around. A breeze blows over your form, twitching the ragged remains of your torn clothes. At the cervical vertebra is a formation of white pus. It turns red and starts to mushroom into a small, pinkish balloon. As it expands, it sprouts orifices. A small, pointy snout for a nose, little leaf shapes for ears, slits for closed eyelids, and a bulb for the mouth. From thousands of follicles, shock-white gray hair comes out. Restored to full size, your mouth pops open with an exhale, making a sound, "Pahhh!" Your eyes blink. The skin tone returns to your normal pale white flesh, and you now have a complete replacement head.

From the upper vertebra at the rib cage of your levitating body, a thin drop of whitish fluid elongates down to the lumbar vertebra. It connects and seals. Growing thicker, it reforms all the vertebra and cartilage. Nerves and blood vessels at first hair thin begin to thicken and branch out. Small polyps for each organ, stomach, kidneys, liver, and pancreas grow into fullness adhered to and hanging from the diaphragm. From the stomach squiggles out an intestine, lowering like a worm the distance of the abdomen and connecting to its appropriate orifice, the anus. As it elongates, it stacks up into place until lower, upper, and duodenum pressurize into form. Abdominal muscle then begins as threads and forms solidly. A membrane glistens over the muscle, transparent at first and becomes opaque as it thickens into skin. Shirt material unfolds like a Venetian blind where it was torn. You think to move your arm to tuck the shirt in. After a long pause you do so, also closing your jacket and buttoning it, then raising your fist to your mouth to cover a slight cough. You have been restored, hair in place, fresh in your clean business suit.

However, you are not happy. Everything is exactly the same. There has been no change, and you know there will be none coming. Having been blown to pieces and remolded served no purpose at all. As the clouds roll through the blue sky overhead, the breeze hits your eyes, causing the same dryness you feel every day as you blink. Your mind repeats the same question it does many times in the waking hours of each day. The question is, "What are you supposed to feel?"

You only feel MORBIDITY.

The next scene appears. You are over a cliff, looking out over the ocean. At the base of the cliff, you can barely make out waves crashing against the rock through the haze, the sound not audible because it is drowned out by the constant ringing in your head. Your body is still levitated, your feet in air a short distance over rock. Suddenly, the rock—having been only painted Styrofoam in a rectangular section—drops downward on hinges. Slowly at first, you descend. Gaining speed, you smell stench as cold mist surrounds.

Deeper and faster, then slowing onto a graveyard, tombstones, and dogs. Their howls you hear loud and clear.

MORBIDITY.

Again you awake. Frozen with panic, you cry and pray; this time the dream is over. Head is a ball of broken, powdery aspirin. Formaldehyde thick in the blood vessels, moving slow. Throat dry like the preserved remains of a mummy. Thoughts become words, and words dissipate into meaninglessness. Canary reach out contrition longitude, glazing the iceberg, shall implode all horizons into one compact atmosphere. Tomorrow blinded, letters burned, gifts stomped. In the next segment, a ghost so hazy. Weeks ahead, bodies frying, riots. For hope of the future a toast is made by the hand and blown to pieces with gunshot.

As the glass crashes to the table in slo-mo, the hand bleeds and the phalange bones are exposed to cold air. You cannot get out of bed from paralysis. Taking time to think depletes energy. The arms are stiff, and the hands are tingling, numb from what they've been grabbing, which is nothing. To become vertical is impossible.

MORBIDITY.

Now your feet are walking on concrete past others in their usual business attire. You actually had woken up in the morning and gone to work as usual. However, your day had been so meticulously similar to every day that you passed through it, with the illusion that you were still in bed and couldn't get out. The paperwork, people's voices, and diversion inside and outside buildings in no way distracted your attention from your constant state of subvert concentration and the grotesque theater playing in your mind.

Oceans darker, minds polluted, greed consuming the clouds. The same day as before has been traveled, no battles won, no borders crossed, all a debilitating séance. Thoughts become words, and words dissipate into an obliterated meaninglessness. If vision befalls decadence, all attempts meandering painfully decided the distinct god pills above. Memory a haze, nothing important known in the past, the buildings, slight changes, however unimportant and mundane. Friends gone, leaving bleak white walls to talk to. The schoolyards, smaller, squarer, more murderous. Inside of a chain-link fence is a beehive of small savages, tumultuous, chaotic, and growing more treasonous by the second.

From first sin comes one better. From thin poison comes one thicker.

From last addiction comes deadly suffocation. From pitch-black comes darkness darker.

From deep space comes coldness colder. From root evil comes horror more horrible.

From strangled throats come screams much louder. At the middle is a dissecting plane of monotony.

At the extremities is an opaque vagueness stretching into the blackness of infinity.

At the core, twisting tighter is MORBIDITY.

The Afterlife

Life begins and is lived. Beliefs are developed during its stages. A surprise is included in every life, and all know when the surprise happens. At death. In the afterlife, all beliefs morally defined by man are erased. Visual awareness becomes a cube shape. Next to visual awareness is another cube shape wherein a three-dimensional movie of the life lived is played. This two-cube shape exists in black space with nothing else, the space stretching into infinity.

The movie that plays differs from the life that was lived in that characters thoughts can be heard, showing the truth that existed during life.

For instance, in a scene where a wife's face is close up to visual awareness she says, "I love you," but her thought is heard, *However, I love the man I've been having an affair with more.*

An employer's remark that is remembered is, "You're a good man and a valuable asset," but the thought heard at the same time is, *You're a simple buffoon and I would never want to be you.*

Memories of making love with the wife are shown in the cube, but in the proximity of her head are scenes of what she was always visualizing: other men. A businessman who was chairman of a board of executives can see scenes of when he was at work, behind walls that fade to transparency and the volumes of people's voices audible…

"How boring is the old crony going to be today?" "Don't worry, he's got to croak sometime."

A man that lived the life of a simple worker such as a mechanic and never received a higher education is shown a scene he was not aware of during his life in which his wife is on the phone to a friend…

"I'm embarrassed to be in a crowd of people like that. My husband is just so dumb, and he wouldn't know what to talk about."

A judge who tried a homicide case in which the defendant was found not guilty sees a scene where the man is torturing the victim. While the victim fights and screams the murderer blurts out, "I'm going to kill you in cold blood and get away with it!"

The victim's eyes roll back in their head, and they die. Every incorrect verdict the judge tried in his courtroom is shown to him during his afterlife movie, making a farce out of his career, his life.

A woman who died lonely and old sees scenes in which people she knew at work are at parties commenting that...

"It wouldn't have been right to invite her, she's just so out of it."

A president sees scenes in offices of the White House in which top cabinet members are speaking frankly among themselves.

"We all know the real decisions are being made by you and me. The country would fall apart if the only man making decisions were the president. He is virtually a simple oaf."

A man sees his parents talking earnestly during his boyhood. The mother to the father, "We should not have had a third child," with a look of sincere resignation in her face.

Every superficial circumstance that existed during the lifespan is revealed, scene by scene. The truth.

The entire life is shown as it progressed, day by day, until the end. Then it starts over again. This is the afterlife of people who lived superficial lives. Their soul is eternally imprisoned within that cube, viewing the paradoxes of their life in the other cube, repetitively revealed their insignificance and unable to contest or respond in any way, in a void without gravity or sense of touch, taste, or smell, with only the senses of sight and sound, in a blackness which continues into infinity. For them, this is eternity.

For those people whose lives were graced with the ultimate fortune of cinematic stardom, the afterlife is this. After death, the conscious creeps awake restored first with the sense of sight. What is seen is a bleak, white concrete surface which continues into infinity, the afterlife floor. It is smooth and plain with no dents, cracks, lines, or marks. Perpendicular to the floor is a wall of the same flawless concrete, which reaches vertically into infinity. The air is filled a thin mist so visibility does not reach farther than about forty yards looking up against the wall or out over the floor.

The body is restored in good health at the age in which the superstar was most famous. John Wayne, Carey Grant, Katheryn Hepburn, Jack Nicholson, Arnold Schwarzenneger, Julia Roberts, Sylvester Stallone, Denzel Washington, Micheal Douglas, Jane Fonda, James Dean, Marilyn Monroe, Humphry Bogart, and all others who made a fortune as cinematic stars are there. The dead movie stars of fame. If they are still living, then they are destined to arrive there and join the others in their afterlife.

Each star wears a plain white cotton overalls clean suit that never gets dirty, along with plain white shoes. There is no jewelry, and the women have no makeup. There is no individuality. All are the same. They rarely speak to each other, and there is nothing special about being them. There are no fans to ask for autographs or give them a sense of flattery. They walk slowly, aimlessly, in one direction for long periods of time—in the former life what would have been days and weeks—only to change their direction in futility, never finding anything different. Stepping aside, they file past each other, moving like zombies with expressionless faces.

The wall is very gradually curved so that if one walks alongside it for a great length of time, they return to the original point, but there are no distinguishing markings of any kind, and a starting point can never be discerned to use as a destination. This leaves them with only a vague, limited sense of space of their surroundings. Many of them wonder if they will ever find a way to measure the wall. Many of them are aware that it is circular, having arrived at the conclusion that they are walking in circles. Although the curve is more gradual than what can be seen through the mist, they have noticed the subtle angle of their walking using their sense of direction. The wall is a vast cylinder reaching up into infinity. It is impossible to reach its top; they think as they stare upward—it has no top.

The alternative to walking alongside the wall is to venture outward on the floor. Many of them do so, fading out into the mist in one direction for great lengths of time, losing the crowd at the wall. They find nothing but solitude, more floor, more even mist, soundlessness, and nothingness. Eventually, they change direction and arrive back at the wall, joining a slow, continuous motion of people moving in either direction.

They had lived their lives in the cradle of fame, full of themselves with ultimate celebrity ego. In the afterlife, they see that there is nothing at all special about any one of them and that they had simply lived very lucky lives. The only meaning in the shape of the wall and the floor is that it is vaguely symbolic of the inside of a film reel, the floor being the flat metal side and the wall being the cylinder of the inside of a reel. They move on and on, recognizing each other but never feeling the need to speak another's name.

John Travolta, Tom Cruise, Nichole Kidman, Bruce Willis, Meryl Streep, Burt Reynolds, Brad Pitt, Clint Eastwood, Charles Bronson, Steven Sagal, Robert Deniro, Al Pacino, Dustin Hoffman, Marlon Brando. Seeing each other's faces arouses no interest as they move past each other in perpetual motion and in constant unchanging light with no night or day. They never get tired or feel pain. They never get hungry or eat. They never sit, lie down, or sleep. They only walk. Walk forever. Walk. This is their eternity.

The destiny of those who became tattered vagrants and wasted their lives on frequent alcoholic binges begins after they die of heart failure, liver disease, or any condition that can be brought on after years of ravaging the body with toxic alcoholic consumption. The eyes open to see a long, white line on black asphalt. Breathing difficultly and coughing, his head raises up from cold, hard, and gritty pavement to see next to the white line a pair of shiny black boots. Police boots. Standing.

"Get up and walk the white line," he hears from a deep, loud, and slightly echoing voice. Grumbling, he stumbles to his feet, arduously picking himself up with his arms and painfully scraping his knees.

Standing, he blinks his eyes as he rocks back and forth on his heels, the middle ear swimming with the imbalance of drunkenness. The only thing he sees is the pulsating image of the white line, continuing into the distance of infinity.

"Huhnn?" he says through the tattered, unkempt beard and mustache. The skin of his face and hands is soiled and wrinkled. His clothes are dirty rags torn with holes and his shoes worn through and falling apart. He squints with one eye, trying to focus and see the distance of the line. He turns about, and it stretches on forever in the other direction. He grumbles in disgust and tries to walk off to the side and away from it, but after only a few steps he loses his balance, falling painfully to the asphalt, and gasps out, "Awww."

When he awakes after having passed out, his face is looking down the same white line again. He hears again, "Get up and walk the white line."

Seeing the huge, shiny black boots once again right in front of his head, he stumbles to his feet; but as he stands blinking, there is no one there. He looks up skyward, holding his shifting balance with his arms out. There is no sky. Nothing, only blackness. Only the asphalt and the white line can be seen illuminated by light having an origin that can't be seen or found. He once again tries to walk off of the line and escape it but loses balance, falling painfully to the pavement and passing out again. When he comes to once again, his face is directly on that same white line, and the police boots are there.

"Get up and walk the white line."

He screams, "Noooo!" as he stands up and tries to run but falls flat on his face again, blurting out in pain, "Aaaughgh!"

Every time he tries to get up and walk off the line, he loses gravity and the pavement jumps up to slam him in the face with a thud. In and out of consciousness, the same boots are there next to his head with the same loud voice, "Get up and walk the white line."

And that same white line. Sobbing, he stands again and again. Every time he stands up, no police man can be found. When finally he does walk forward on the line, he gets about ten steps, able to steady himself using the line as a visual guide to place one foot in front of the other. Still he falls in his drunken stupor and passes out. The asphalt rocks back and forth as he takes some staggering steps, then lurches upward to clobber him.

This is the wino's simplistic, endless cycle. He remains on a drunken binge that never ends, sobriety never to come again, with the futile, perpetual attempting of standing straight to walk forward, failing, collapsing and becoming unconscious, then regaining conscious.

If veering from the line, then the boots and the voice after falling and waking up as a reminder to always stay on that same white line. It is for eternity.

You awake. You just died and find yourself lying on a floor next to a long wooden staircase. It goes up farther than you can see. Other than the staircase, there is nothing but a black floor continuing out beyond your range of vision, fading into darkness. You begin to walk up the stairs. Step after step, you climb, resting and then continuing. There is a railing, and every twenty-five steps, a lightbulb hanging from a wire. You climb what seems to be forever, hoping to find a doorway or a floor, but only steps continue.

Looking down, you can't see anything but the staircase. You wonder how far you've come. There has to be a top, you think. However, no matter how high you climb, there is only more steps. In a fit of madness, you stand up on the railing and grab the lightbulb hanging from the wire. The wire snaps, and sparks spit from it as the lightbulb burns out. Falling backward, you hit the staircase heavily. Tumbling down, you scream as your head, back, arms, and legs collide with the hard wooden stairs. You gain speed as you descend, breaking knees, ribs, femurs, forearms, pelvic, elbows, and cranium. Nearly every bone is broken as you scream in pain, reverberating loudly against the wooden steps. However, you remain completely conscious until finally hitting the floor at the bottom.

You roll over in pain with your arms and torso twisted unnaturally, sprawled on the floor. For a long time you cannot stand up. Then you begin to feel strange sensations in all the places where your bones are broken. Each bone moves gently into place and fuses, healing as you writhe gently on the floor. Restored to full health, you stand up, breathing steadily in and out. You make the decision to walk out into the distance on the floor away from the staircase.

Nothing can be seen except complete blackness. No sound can be heard other than your constant footsteps on the wooden floor. You look back to see the dimly lit staircase, rising up higher than you can visually comprehend, into infinity. After a timely trek continuing in the direction away from the staircase, you find nothing and decide to turn back. In the distance you can still see a single point of light, which must be the staircase. You start back.

You have nothing but time to reflect back on your former life. You had always tried to get somewhere to improve your status but never could. You never could buy the things you wanted. You never could afford to travel to the places you dreamed of. Your life was lived in one place: your boring hometown.

Everything you owned was always much more modest than you fantasized about. You watched the lifestyles of the rich and famous every day on television and in magazines. You died never achieving near what you dreamed of.

Arriving back at the staircase, you begin your endless climb. There is nothing else to do. Hope drives you upward. Every step you take, holding your head up to see as far as you can, clutching the railing with your hand, you hope to see anything different. But you never will. The staircase reaches into infinity. This is the afterlife of those who always dreamed of getting somewhere in life but never could. For them, it is eternity.

Imagine a man whose life is so mundane and monotonous that he doesn't live at all; he only exists.

Renting a stark, small room in a tenement house by the week, he works through a temporary labor service at a warehouse. As he comes to work each day, he greets the other coworkers, knowing nothing more about them than their names and never finding anything more in common with them. At quitting time, he rides the van back to the temporary agency, which is just a room with chairs and a counter behind, which the clerk is always writing on tickets and giving directions. On the window at the front, in bold letters it says, "Wanted, Temporary Help." Other than that, there is only the door, which locks after six o'clock and opens again before dawn.

He walks the rest of the way home to his boarding room. The walls up the stairways have cracks and chipped paint. Cigarette butts are on the stairs and the concrete stairwells. The hallways are cold and drafty with taped, cracked windows dirty enough to barely see the street lamps on the sidewalk outside. Unlocking a creaky wooden door—which has a lumpy surface from being painted many, many times—he turns on the single exposed lightbulb. There is an old metal spring bed, a small black-and-white TV, a window through which cold air seeps badly, an old dresser drawer with all his clothes and belongings, a small sink worn down to the metal where the water runs, above it a small spotted mirror, and a tile floor with several broken tiles revealing a wooden layer underneath.

He has no friends. He has no family. What family he had once, he stopped communicating with years ago; others died. He spends his time watching his small TV, never going out to clubs, concerts, or events. His clothes are all secondhand, bought at bleak thrift stores. He owns nothing of value. For Christmas Eve and New Year's Eve, he usually buys a few bottles of hard liquor and celebrates alone in his room, inebriated with the TV running, staring at the cold outside through the window.

After a year or so, he will quit his job at the warehouse or be fired; then he will set out to find another low-paying, mundane job. After a few years, he will become curious as to what might be different in a new city, pack his things in a few shoulder bags, and take a bus there. He finds the exact same life with a low-paying job and a cheap room in a tenement building. He has moved from city to city, until it all seems the same. He will always have this same stark existence wherever he goes.

What this man can't be sure of is if he is, in fact, alive at all. Every few years, he wakes up in the creaky bed of his cold room to find that time has jumped back a matter of years. As he walks down a sidewalk and sees the date on a newspaper in a stand, bewilderment sets in. He remembers it has happened before, and before that. He becomes mortified, feeling a great insecurity of being stuck in the reality of a bizarre time warp. But there is no one he can tell, having no friends, and no one to confide in. His life is a blur with no starting point and a repeating cycle that prevents an end from ever coming.

He actually did die long, long ago as he slept in his bed, having drunk an incredible amount of alcohol on New Year's Day. His afterlife is exactly the same monotony that his life had been with the twist of jumping back in time a period of every few years. Those who became completely alone and friendless, existing on the fringe of obscurity, are transferred to this bleak realm after death. They are destined to experience their own isolated monotony in an unending repeating cycle, forever. For the tenement house man, when the twist happens, he panics and tries to find a way to become free, remembering that it has happened endless times before. But there is nothing he can do and no one he can talk to. After time has passed by again, month after month, he stops thinking about it and convinces himself that it did not happen and things are normal.

He may move to another city, take on another low-paying job in another plain, old factory and move into a different room in another cheap boarding house, but he will never break the cycle. Buying clothes in dark old thrift stores, shuffling through the lonely streets at night, buying groceries in markets and convenient stores with clerks that recognize him but take no interest in him personally, never meeting friends, never having fun, he exists. He exists for eternity.

Then there are those who lived lives of fulfillment, love, and joy. They played energetically in childhood, having many friends, parents who cared about them, a safe and warm home and a fascination for life. As young people, they had healthy relations with the opposite sex. In school, they learned to compete and excel. Some went on to higher education and became doctors, helping others during their lives. Others became scholars, businesspeople, scientists, and experts. Some excelled at sports and became athletes. This type of person lived a life with something they delved into—a fascination, something they were good at.

They met the one they fell in love with and married, raising children. Changes in their lives never conquered them as they adapted to always win. Their friends and family were many and always glad to hear from them. They loved their children, and the children loved them back, growing up to carry on tradition. They lived good lives.

At death is a long passageway with brilliant light. At the end of the passageway is a library with perfect, high ceilings; beautiful golden carpet; and fantastic, ornate wooden walls and shelves. In the library, it is completely quiet, and a soul walking through is completely alone. The books on the shelves are a chronological listing of all the events of the days of the life of that person. Feeling a surge of excitement and happiness, the soul removes one of the large books from the shelves. In it are pictures with every small detail of that period of life. The soul puts it down onto a huge, beautiful wooden table in the middle of the floor and, sitting in a huge wooden chair that looks like a king's throne, begins reading, thumbing through chapter to chapter, remembering all the circumstances of their life.

Book after book is retrieved from the shelves as all the fond memories are relived from pictures on page after page. The pictures show everything: the first baby's birth, the bride and groom at the altar, the girl or boy of a childhood crush sitting in a chair in class, the mother outside the old house from childhood, Dad driving the old car, the dog running through the yard. Each memory brings back all types of feelings as a soul relives their life. The soul can stay in the library as long as it wants, turning the pages of the books, reading the details, forgotten moments and quotes, gazing mesmerized at the true life pictures and remembering.

When the soul is satisfied, a large doorway opens up at the other end of the library. The soul walks over and stands at the doorway. There are two passageways. At the end of one is a scene of a mother in maternity in a hospital room, about to have a baby. The other passageway continues into the distance so that the end can't be seen.

A voice is heard, "You can either live again by walking down this passageway, or you go on to something different by walking down the other passageway."

You can reincarnate into a similar life with a different mother and different people and places. It will be a good life, like the one you lived. The other option is to walk down the other passageway on to something unknown, something different. As you stand at the doorway resolute, you take all the time in the world, weighing the alternatives to make the decision you feel right about. Because you lived a good life, in your afterlife you have a choice. Which will be your eternity?

When They *Les Miserables*

Officer Keeth and Officer Reed were the pedestal of their precinct, having spent fourteen years on the force walking a beat downtown. They knew everything that happened. They were familiar with all the characters in the inner city: the pimps, the drug dealers. They knew all the trouble areas. There were alleyways where drug abuse, prostitution, and violence took place frequently. There were dive bars where fights broke out usually on Saturday night, necessitating physical arrests with backup called on the walkie-talkie. Keeth and Reed made more arrests than anyone in their unit, and they were the most respected.

Among the many trouble areas downtown was an alley next to a homeless shelter that was almost always strewn with vagrants sleeping in cardboard boxes at night. For years it had been that way. The police couldn't clear them out. Citizens were frequently hassled for money or robbed by vagrants walking by the alley. Keeth and Reed referred to it as the "Dog Pound." They both held a particular contempt for homeless vagrants, the shelter itself, or anything to do with homelessness. Years before, Keeth's sixteen-year-old daughter, Lisa, had met a nineteen-year-old homeless young man named Victor, who was somewhat of a jack of all trades and a traveler from California. Keeth's relationship with his daughter had always been jaded by the fact that he was a police officer, and Lisa felt she could never be cool with her friends at school. On a summer day, she was walking through the park downtown, only blocks from the Dog Pound, and she met Victor. They took to each other right away, and she agreed to meet him in the park several times in the days ahead. They fell in love and ran away together, hitchhiking across country. Lisa only left a note for her dad on her bed. That was the last he ever saw her.

The next year during the summer, by an astronomical coincidence, the exact same thing happened to Reed. His seventeen-year-old daughter, Andrea, met up with a twenty-year-old young man named Bryce, whom she found playing guitar in the park downtown. She also had wanted to be free from her father, having always hated that he was a police officer. Andrea and Bryce left the city to find whatever was out there, and she called once they were miles away…

"Daddy, I've run away."

He never heard from her again.

On Friday and Saturday nights late, after their shift was over, Keeth and Reed headed to the Rusty Nail, a bar predominated by all their comrade police officers. They would take their seats at the end of the bar in front of a TV and order a pitcher. On one particular Friday late night, they strolled in, sat down, and ordered their usual. On the TV was a late night show: *The Best of Broadway*.

The announcer spoke, "In 1991, what began as a Broadway hit and became one of the most highly regarded plays of its time, *Les Miserables*…"

Keeth took a sip from his glass. The two drank steadily as the show progressed. They began to feel well. A scene was shown in which French peasants sat huddled en masse wearing dirty clothes.

Keeth said, "These people remind me of the Dog Pound." Reed said, "Yeah."

"That whole Dog Pound is the *Les Miserables* crowd." "Yeah."

"You know, I got a good idea for this *Les Miserables* crowd." "Yeah."

"I said, I got a good idea for this *Les Miserables* crowd." "Yeah."

"It is not so much the fact that they are *Les Miserables*'n, but when they." "Aww, right."

"When they *Les Miserables*, beat them. When they *Les Miserables*, stun them. When they *Les Miserables*, kill them!"

Reed looked now at the TV with comprehending eyesight through the haze of beer. The dialog from the play trailed on.

Keeth continued, "When they *Les Miserables*, eliminate them. If and when they *Les Miserables*, gather forces and crush them."

Reed blurted out, "Ha!"

The audible laugh caused the other police sitting down bar to look their way. The two became secretive, lowering their voices.

Keeth said, "When they *Les Miserables*, one might go even so far as to put a Jaws of Life on the neck of one of the *Les Miserables* and 'get medieval' on that certain anatomical area."

Reed took a quick swig from his glass and joined, "May all those who *Les Miserables* be condemned.

Anyone who is caught *Les Miserables*ing or even closely resembling the *Les Miserables* shall be condemned. If even I or you are to *Les Miserables*, then it would be us to suffer the wrath of those administering the punishment."

Keeth said, "When they *Les Miserables*, ruin them. Hey, I got a good idea what we can do tonight, c'mon."

The two left the bar and strolled blocks down the sidewalk. Keeth said, "Let's pay a visit to the Dog Pound."

Reed said, "The Dog Pound, what do ya wanna go there for?" "Just follow me, you'll see."

The two crossed an intersection at the pedestrian walk signal and headed down blocks to their familiar destination, the Dog Pound. Two street lamps on the walls lining the alley shown light up and down it in the still of the night. At this time of night, there was no movement. All the vagrants were asleep under their cardboard boxes and blankets.

Keeth said to Reed, "Now this is how the *Les Miserables* genre should be dealt with."

He reached into a heap of boxes and flung them aside, revealing a curled-up sleeping vagrant who woke with a surprised look on his face. Keeth grabbed him with both hands firmly around the collar and heaved the entire weight of the body to standing position, then shoved the vagrant backward into the wall and held him against it at the shoulders. The vagrant tried to fight but was no match for Keeth's strength.

He said exasperatingly, "What do you want, whu-what did I do?"

Keeth slapped him on both sides of the face and said, "Wake up you *Les Miserables* bum. Wake up!

When they *Les Miserables*, pound them!"

He clenched his right fist, cocked back the arm, and planted a firm punch into the vagrant's gut. The vagrant doubled over and grunted, "Ooooh!"

Reed flung aside some more boxes, grabbed another vagrant wearing dirty, tattered clothes similar to the first, stood him up, and slapped him awake.

He threw the vagrant back against the wall and said, "When they *Les Miserables*, bruise them!" He threw a punch to the gut, and the man doubled over and fell to his knees.

The other vagrants were waking up from the noise down the length of the alleyway, moving their boxes and blankets, sitting up and saying, "What's goin' on?"

"Who's that?" "What's happening?"

Keeth walked over to one, grabbed him at the collar, lifted him up to his feet, shoved him back against the wall, grabbed him at the shoulder, and shoved a stiff knee into his gut. The man tumbled over onto his hands and feet and blurted out, "Aaawww!"

Reed grabbed another one and flung him against the wall then lowered his shoulder, holding his left forearm with his right hand, and shoved the entire weight of his body into the victim's midsection like a football player hitting the padding of a sled on a practice field. The man bounced off of the wall and stumbled to the ground, joining the others groveling on the asphalt. Keeth and Reed were making their way methodically down the length of the entire alley, picking up each individual and pulverizing them.

Two more active ones put up a fight, yelling at the top of their lungs, "Get the hell out of here. Who the hell are you?"

But they were no match for Keeth and Reed's bulk strength and fighting skills, acquired over years of arresting people on Saturday nights. Most of the remaining picked up their belongings and fled, clearing the alley. When Keeth and Reed were finished, they had beaten up about half the men they found there. A few were still struggling on their hands and knees while most had stumbled out of the alley. Keeth and Reed walked to the mouth of the alley, looking back over their work with boxes and blankets left behind.

Keeth threw up his arms and yelled, "When they *Les Miserables*, destroy them! Ha-ha-ha-ha…" They both walked away into the night laughing.

"Hey, we gotta do this again some time," Reed said.

They walked through the empty streets in the darkness and silence of the night back to where their cars were parked at the Rusty Nail, then drove home.

A few days later, after the shift was over, Keeth and Reed found themselves back in their seats in the Rusty Nail, ordering the usual. On the TV came the same show again, *The Best of Broadway*.

The announcer spoke, "In 1984, one of the most popular plays of all time started on Broadway, *Cats*.

First entertaining audiences on Broadway, it went on to travel to major cities all over the country…"

The play progressed as the two drank steadily and began getting a buzz. It came to a scene that showed about a dozen actors dressed in cat costumes repeating a phrase…

"Jelicho cats are jumping and bouncing. Jelicho cats are reaching and climbing. Jelicho cats are dancing and prancing. Jelicho cats are stalking and walking."

"Look at these faggots," Reed said to Keeth. "Every single one of 'em is a faggot."

Keeth said, "The way they're all gathered in that alleyway reminds me of the damage we did at the Dog Pound a few nights ago. Put me and you in there, and these faggots wouldn't stand a chance. We would massacre all of them."

Reed said, "And it wouldn't be Jelicho cats. With one of them in a choke hold, I'd be setting him straight. I'd be telling him as I knee him in the ribs: 'Jelly cats are bouncing and falling.' As I put another in a head grip and cover the mouth and nose so he can't breathe, I'd say to him, 'Jelly cats are tripping and slipping.' As I kick out the knees of another one of those faggot clowns in a cat suit, splattering him on the asphalt, I'd say to him, "Jelly cats are beat up and hurting.'"

Keeth said, "I'd get one of those punk faggots backed up against a wall, slap his face from side to side, then punch the wind out of him in the gut, saying, 'Jelly cats are screaming and running.' Yeah, put me and you in that little scene, and we'd scatter 'em just like we did the Dog Pound a few nights ago. Speaking of the Dog Pound…"

Keeth took his gaze down from the TV screen and looked at Reed. Reed met his gaze. Reed said, "Are you thinking what I'm thinking?"

Keeth said, "Let's go pay the Dog Pound a visit."

The two hastily downed the last of their beer and put the mugs down on the bar with a thud. Reed said, "Let's go kick some jelly cats on their asses."

The two picked up their coats from off of the barstools, put them on, and headed out the door into the cool night air. They walked down the blocks, crossing the empty early-morning streets and arrived at the mouth of the Dog Pound alley. As usual, it was dimly lit by the high-mounted street lamps. Down the length of it were the still, sleeping bodies of about thirty vagrants under boxes and blankets. Keeth and Reed paused for a brief moment in the silence, viewing their target. They burst into a commotion, throwing up their arms and kicking over the boxes of the nearest bums.

Keeth yelled out, "Hey, hey! Wake up! Everybody, wake up! The bum squad is back! Rise and shine!

Everybody up, it's time to party!"

He and Reed uncovered more and more bums, throwing the boxes and blankets down the alley. As the men woke up and moved, Keeth and Reed both grabbed one apiece and jerked them to a standing position.

Reed yelled out as he twisted and cranked the arm behind the back of his man, "Jelly cats are stumbling and fumbling!"

He tripped the vagrant with a foot and sent him falling forward with a shove. Keeth grabbed the long hair tied into a ponytail on his man and made him stumble back and forth by jerking his head backward. He then pulled hard and threw him onto his back. On the ground, he kicked the body over on his stomach and planted a foot hard into the kidney.

The vagrant grunted in pain, "Aaawww-haw-haw!"

Keeth yelled out, "Jelly cats are moaning and groaning!"

Reed grabbed the hair of another one and walked him off-balance halfway bending over, leading him toward the wall, speeding him up, and then throwing him into the wall.

The man blurted out in pain as his arms and head hit the solid brick wall with a heavy thud, "Unh!"

Reed yelled out, "Jelly cats are tripping and limping! Jelly cats are grunting and hurting!"

Keeth picked up another by the back of the collar and held him in a headlock. He smacked him in the face to get him alert, then clasped his hand around the mouth. Moving the jaw up and down and pressing the lips, Keeth tried to get the bum to say the words he was repeating…

"Jelly cats are writhing and groveling! Jelly cats are wreaking and kicking!"

Sure enough, the bum got the point, nodded his head, and blurted out the words, "Jell-jelly cats, juh-jell-jelly cats…"

"There ya go!" said Keeth, and he punched him hard in the gut and threw him down on the asphalt.

Reed picked up another, turned him around, shoved a foot onto his butt and shoved him forward. The vagrant stumbled forward into Keeth's grasp. Keeth turned him around, shoved a foot onto his butt, and shoved him stumbling forward again back to Reed. They were tossing the bum back and forth like a game of catch. When Keeth got tired of shoving the bum back and forth, he caught him stumbling forward with a firm knee into the stomach, doubling him over and flinging him onto the ground with the usual *whump* sound of a body hitting the asphalt. Keeth and Reed played catch with bum after bum, shoving them back and forth a few times and then punching, tripping, or just plain dropping them onto the asphalt. They actually formed somewhat of a temporary pile of bodies, one being dumped onto others slow to get up back onto their feet.

Reed proclaimed, "Jelly cats are falling and piling!"

Occasionally, a more active bum would try to fend for himself, but then Keeth and Reed would gang up on him, overpower him, stun him by method of punch, kick, choke hold, etc., and send him flying headfirst onto the asphalt where the other bums were gathering themselves up and staggering out of the alley. Keeth and Reed came to the last bum at the end of the alley. The rest had run off, clearing out the alley and leaving a scene of boxes and blankets strewn across the ground. They stood there waiting, and he tried to run around them. Reed caught him and choke-held him around the neck. Keeth grabbed onto both legs and picked up his lower body. Reed caught on and clasped him under the armpits. They both swung him back and forth a few times and then said, "One, two, three…" and flung his body into the air.

He landed with a disheartening *thump* onto the asphalt, saying, "Oooowww!"

Reed yelled down the alley, "Jelly cats are flying and collapsing!"

Keeth eyed the empty alleyway and proclaimed triumphantly, "Jelly cats are running their asses off and out of there!"

The two stood at the back of the empty alley, looking down it, congratulating themselves and giving each other a high five.

Reed said, "Now that was some exercise!"

The two walked to the mouth of the alley and looked in both directions down the streets. Some of the bums could be seen walking off into the distance. Keeth and Reed walked back to their parked cars at the Rusty Nail and drove home.

Days later, they were each on patrol, walking the beat in the afternoon. By coincidence, they passed by each other and stopped to greet the other. They were only a few blocks away from the Dog Pound.

Keeth said to Reed, "What say we go rouse 'em up at the Dog Pound, I got nothing else better to do." Reed said, "No way, it's broad daylight and we're in uniform."

Keeth said, "I know. So what? We go in and rouse 'em up. It'll only take twenty minutes. I'm startin' to get addicted to it."

Reed said, "That's what I'm afraid of. You know, Keeth, no matter how much we beat up bums at the Dog Pound, it's not gonna bring back your daughter, Lisa, or my Andrea."

Keeth said, "I know that, but it's a darn good way to take out some aggravation. C'mon, let's go over there and let 'em have it. C'mon."

Keeth started walking in the direction of the Dog Pound alley, and Reed reluctantly followed. At the Dog Pound was a gathering of vagrants sitting with their backs against the wall lined up and down the alley.

One was saying to some others, "There's been these two guys that come at night and beat up people. They harass everyone so bad that people leave and find somewhere else to sleep. I got punched in the gut and thrown to the ground. It wasn't fun. One guy said he heard them call themselves the Bum Squad. I don't know what their problem is or what kind of vigilante kick their on, but they're gonna get in trouble doing what they're doing, sooner or later."

Just then Keeth and Reed appeared at the mouth of the alley and stood with authority, holding their clubs.

Keeth yelled out full volume, "OK, grubs. Everybody up on their feet. Let's go. Move it!" Reed yelled out, "Time to play people. Time to play!"

The two moved in on the nearest man as they all stood up. Keeth grabbed him, turned him around, and shoved him against the wall. The man stood with his hands against the wall and his legs spread apart expecting to be searched, but Keeth grabbed him at the back of his collar, jerked him backward, pointed him in the direction of the sidewalk outside the alley, and shoved him forward, saying, "Get out of here!"

Keeth and Reed began grabbing each one of them and shoving them in the direction to vacate the alley. If they put up the slightest resistance, then they got a club to the ribs or the jaw.

The vagrant that had been talking to the others about Keeth and Reed said to them, "It's them. They're the ones that have been coming here at night. They're cops!"

Keeth was having a hard time with one struggling against him. He twisted his arm behind his back and said, "You *Les Miserables*'n bum. When they Les *Miserables*, force them!"

Keeth shoved his police club into the bum's lower back to set him in motion of vacating the alley.

Reed came to the group that had been in conference about him and Keeth. The bum that recognized him from the night time campaigns said, "We're on our way, Officer. We're cooperating in full."

He and his comrades grabbed their baggage and hurried their way out. He peered at Reed's name tag and read it, making sure to remember it. As he passed by Keeth, he made the same observance of his name tag. Reed grabbed ahold of the arm of a vagrant not moving fast enough and hit him on the shoulder with the club, then the back of the head.

He said, "Jelly cats are whining and crawling! Jelly cats are ducking and dodging!"

Keeth had the last few stragglers at the back of the alley. He did free-arm swings with the club, hitting them in the heads and shoulders. He yelled out, "When they *Les Miserables*, batter them!"

The alley finished clearing out with the last bums shuffling out and down the sidewalk, holding their belongings. Keeth and Reed walked to the mouth of the alley and watched the group dissipate. Reed said to Keeth, "That didn't take long at all."

The two walked the opposite direction down the sidewalk and split up back to their regular beats at the intersection. The bum that had recognized them and taken their names was organizing the other two to walk with him to the precinct headquarters and complain.

He said, "I got their names. Reed and Keeth. C'mon, let's find someone that knows where the police station is. Those two can't get away with what they've been doing. We'll get them in trouble. They're not supposed to be beating up people and hassling them."

The three of them walked up to a taxi driver and got the directions to the police station. It wasn't a long walk. When they got there, they walked through the doors and up to a tall counter with an officer on duty.

He said, "What can I do for you?"

The spokesman said, "We want to complain about two police officers beating up people and hassling them in the alley next to the Saint Francis of Assisi Homeless Shelter on Wheeler Street. It just happened about a half hour ago. They came in and started hitting people with their clubs. They made everyone leave. I've been there late at night when the same thing happened. The same two police officers beat people up and cleared out the alley when people were sleeping there. It was the same two officers both times. Today I saw their name tags and remembered them—Officer Keeth and Officer Reed. They're both getting away with police brutality, and we think they should get in trouble."

The officer at the counter, of course, recognized the names of the old workhorses Keeth and Reed. He wrote down some notes on a pad in front of him. He said, "So you say an Officer Keeth and an Officer Reed have been beating people in the alley next to the Saint Francis Homeless Shelter. And it has happened more than once. It happened once at night, is that so?"

"Yes."

"You know that people are not supposed to sleep there, right?"

"Well, yeah."

"OK, gentlemen, thanks for coming in."

The three of them left out the big doors they had entered. The officer behind the counter got on the phone and dialed the captain.

The captain answered, "Captain Lynch speaking."

"Captain, I just had three homeless gentlemen in here telling me that Officers Keeth and Reed have taken on a new hobby—beating up vagrants in the alleyway next to the Saint Francis Homeless Shelter. They say it has happened a number of times, the latest of which was just today about a half hour ago."

The captain said, "Is that so? Well, this sounds interesting. I'll have to have a talk with them. Thanks." He hung up.

When the day shift was over and Keeth and Reed had walked back to the precinct headquarters, they were told at the door to see the captain in his office. Reed had arrived a little while before Keeth and was sitting in a chair in front of the captain's desk.

The captain said, "Keeth, have a seat. Now that I've got you both in here, I'll just let you have it straight. It came to my attention today that several individuals visited the station after they said that they were beat up and chased out of an alley next to that homeless shelter on Wheeler Street. They said that it has happened a number of times and that the two officers involved are Keeth and Reed. They read your name tags guys. Now, what's going on here? Do you have any explanation for your behavior, either of you?"

Keeth and Reed tried to find something to say, guilt written in the looks on their faces.

Keeth spoke up, "It's that damn alley next to the shelter. There's always bums there. It's been there too long, and no one has done anything about it."

The captain pointed his finger at Keeth from across the desk and said, "That's horseshit, Keeth. You don't take it upon yourself to initiate the kind of action you did. If I wanted something done about that area, I would have planned it. Me. I'm the one giving orders at this precinct. Do you have anything to say for yourself?" He looked at Reed from across the desk.

Reed said, "Captain, I know what we did was wrong, and we won't do it again."

"You're darn right you won't do it again. I can't remember the last time either of you was in this office for a reprimanding, you've both always been clean as long as I can remember. But I can't let this go unpunished. You're both suspended for three days. That'll give you time to think. Did this occurrence have anything to do with the fact that both your daughters ran away with homeless men several years ago?" He stared at them across the desk but got no answer. He said, "Well, take three days off, and think about it. I'll see you in uniform next week, gentlemen. That's all."

Keeth and Reed left the office solemnly. They went to the locker room and changed into their civilian clothes.

Reed said to Keeth, "Well, it was fun while it lasted."

Keeth said, "Hey, it ain't over. We can find some other way to keep hassling them. Maybe we can find them in the park at night, when our shift is over and we're not in uniform. Going in there in uniform was our mistake. It was my idea. Sorry. It's a big city. I'm sure we can find other bums to rouse up."

Reed said, "You gotta be jokin'. I learned my lesson. It's over for me."

The two walked out of the station in plainclothes, toward their cars in the parking lot. Reed got in his as Keeth strolled toward the back of the lot. In the warm spring late afternoon sun, Keeth felt that it wasn't the end but only the beginning. He knew Reed would come around. It would be on a night after drinking at the Rusty Nail; they would get in the right mood and go bum-hunting. Three days suspension and back to the grind. No biggie. They were the Bum Squad. Once it started, you couldn't just call it quits. There were plenty of bums out there roaming around at night, and Keeth and Reed were from now on going to be on the prowl to find them.

Worse Than Kitsch

Go to hell! No, I really mean that—go to hell! You and your generic, plain, all-American image. You make up the mainstream. You're the average family with husband, wife, two kids, two cars, and a house with a yard that you mow on Saturday. There are millions just like you doing the exact same thing as you—living the exact same lives. If you're not living the American dream, at least you're living the American doing. OK. You're the most common, average folk living clean lives and raising children. Since you are the average and the majority, your vote counts the most. There's just one catch: don't even think about trying to do something original. Whatever you do and whatever you can dream of will have been done hundreds of times, way even before you were there to think of it. Your actions in your daily lives, the way you talk, the jokes you make to your friends, and the clothes you wear are all being done, said, told, and worn by hundreds of other people just like you everywhere, every day. Nothing you do will ever be anywhere close to original. You can't be original because you're just too common.

You—the average, mainstream, gullible consumer making up the vast consumer market—are the reason I exist. I am commercialism. I am a constant, a continuum. I've been around ever since radio was invented. With television, I took flight. The mass media would be able to reach into millions of households, advertising every product thinkable. And with every advertisement comes a cheap, commercial spiel that is unworthy of being thought of as invention. A simple phrase is made for everything that is sold, and it is not meant to be artistic or even have any aesthetic value whatsoever; it is only meant to be remembered easily and rather subconsciously so that a person will buy the product. This is where I come into the picture. I am that commercial spiel. I am that cheap, meaningless phrase. You've been listening to me ever since you were born. I've sold you everything from hot dogs to paper towels to soda to automobiles. I sold you your insurance, your house, your clothes, and even your personal hygiene supply. You can go ahead and think of me as immortal. I'll be around eons from now in the future when mankind is flying spaceships to other planets. I'll probably always be around until the end of time. There will always be the need for common advertisement. This is my job. I'll tell you every little catchphrase you've ever heard. I'll give you slogans that you'll repeat to yourself when you're driving down the highway. Any cheesy jingle unworthy of being elevator music was made by me…

This is what I think of the whole system of promotion, the whole being of advertising, the whole realm of commercialism—it can go to hell and die! The people I work with are as superficial as the thirty-second commercials we make. It's always get this done, get that done, hurry up, and make the deadline. In all my years of being in the business, I have never been asked anything about my personal life. None of the people I work with give a damn about me personally, and I can truly say that I have loathed every single person I've ever worked with: every writer, every company representative, every cameraman, on down to even the common crap-eating stage hand meandering around the set. They can all go to hell and die! I have no friends, not to mention any family. This is the reality of being the icon of hokey, worthless advertising. My usual Christmas Eve celebration is getting smashed with a bottle of hard liquor in a cockroach-infested slum of a hotel. It ain't pretty being me…

Let me describe to you my typical workday. I walk into the set with people moving chairs and what not around the stage, actors holding their manuscripts with their lines and reading them, other people motioning to them saying "let's get started" and as usual everything running behind schedule. I grab my copy of the manuscript off of a desk and take a look at it.

"All right, I see what we're dealing with here. Well, here I am, everyone. We can start now."

Not that anyone gives a damn. There are a few groans, and people sit in a circle with some chairs. The manuscript has singers, prerecorded music backup, a guy on an electric guitar, and an announcer. It is a commercial for a car.

I say, "OK, has everyone read their part? Think you can handle it? OK, let's give it a shot."

We all stand up, the chairs are cleared, and microphones are arranged for the singers. The guy with the guitar plugs into a long chord and strums some notes, adjusting the volume. People behind thick glass in the sound booth fix recording panels and nod OK.

I motion to the people in the booth and say, "OK, let's hear the background music. Everyone watch the monitor."

The symphonic music begins as the video for the commercial plays on monitor screens for everyone to see. It lasts thirty seconds.

I say, "All right, now do we know what we're dealing with? Get ready to record. Ready? Three, two, one, and go…"

I point at the singers on the microphones, the backup music starts, and they start singing, Ride with the wind

Fly like a bird Over the mountain

The Stallion's the word

The video shows a sports utility vehicle driving on a dirt road through a desert with a cloud of dust kicking up behind it. The electric guitar starts playing notes, and the announcer does the voice-over…

And now get $5,000 factory rebate on the 2004 Stallion at your local dealer, while they last…

Ride with the wind Fly like a bird Over the mountain

The Stallion's the word

The music and the video come to an end. Everyone cheers and congratulates themselves. I say, "Not so fast, people, that's just the first take. We'll have to do it over and over to get the sound right, c'mon now. You in the middle, what's your name, honey?"

The woman standing at the microphone says, "Barbie Johnson."

"OK, Barbie. Let's do some singing here. You're sounding like a sick cow." "Let's see you sing it, you fat creep."

"That's right, I'm fat, I'm short, and I'm bald. There's more lovable me to go around. Let's do it again, people. This time, try sounding better than a flock of geese stuck in an oil spill."

The backup and the video come on again, and another take is done. Then another. And another. So many takes are done that everyone becomes literally sick of repeating their part.

I yell out, "You're all still sounding like you're bent over a toilet bowl sick to your stomachs. C'mon, I wanna hear some energy."

One of the singers, a man, blurts out, "Go stick it in your ear! We're singing the best that we can."

I say, "Not that any of you can sing. Don't give yourself any delusions of grandeur, pal—you were just what was available on such short notice. A roomful of starving, whining puppies could harmonize better than you, people. C'mon, let's do it again, from the top."

More takes are done until finally I say, "That's a wrap."

Everyone groans with relief, throwing their manuscript in the trashcan as they walk out of the area. It is usually by this time of day that I'm in such a chipper mood I could be in a Walt Disney cartoon. I leave the area with the attitude—now that that's over, screw it. I shove my way into the next stage area and take charge. I grab a manuscript off of the desk and read it.

"Mortenson's Pepperoni Pizza Bites. Not just for snacking—you can make a whole meal out of them!" The stage is set with a kitchen area, a mother-type in an apron, a boy that's supposed to be her son,

and a cookie sheet full of Mortenson's Pepperoni Pizza Bites by an open oven. I hear someone standing behind the camera say, "Everyone, ready, go." The mother motions with the cookie sheet like she is bringing it out of the oven, holding it with an oven mitt and holding the door of the oven with the other hand.

She sees the boy standing there and says, "Here Joey, you're just in time for some Mortenson's Pepperoni Pizza Bites. They're not just good to eat, they're good for you. There's enough here for your whole dinner."

The boy says, "Gee, thanks, Mom." He takes a Pizza Bite off the tray, shoves it in his mouth and says,

"Mmmm, yum."

The mom says, "Mortenson's Pepperoni Pizza Bites. Not just for snacking—you can make a whole meal out of them!"

The background music crescendos with singers harmonizing, "It's always fresh from Mortenson's bakery…"

The camera goes off, and everyone shifts.

I say out loud over the crowd, "OK, I can see we're going to be here awhile. Mom, you and Joey have to act like you know each other. The way you're talking to each other is like someone is holding giant Q cards right in front of your faces. There's no life in either of you. C'mon now, and make it believable. Let's do it again. Ready? Go."

Another take is done, and after the background music cuts off, I wave off the camera and say, "That's better, Mom and Joey, but you're still not making me believe that you're mother and son. You're still talking to each other like strangers."

Just then, the guy handling the camera butts in with his two cents' worth, "I didn't see anything wrong with that take. I say it's a good one."

I look over in his direction, holding my copy of the manuscript. I say, "Who the hell are you, buddy, and just what started making you think your opinion counts around here?"

He says, "It just looked to me like the take was as good as we need. I can't see anything wrong with it, and there's no reason to keep doing it over. We can use the last one."

Now I'm pissed off. I stomp over to him and lurch right up in his face. I raise my voice while shaking my finger in his face, "You don't give orders around here, buddy, I do. I don't care what you think of the take, we're going to do it over and over until I say it's right, is that understood? Just who are you, anyway? Are you new around here? I've been doing this since you were wearing teddy bear pajamas to bed. Now, we're going to start over, and if I want your opinion, Mr. Cameraman, I'll ask for it. By the way, I don't want your opinion."

I walk back to my place outside the camera angle and start them over again. After a few more takes, we finally get it right. I give my "That's a wrap" and walk out of the stage area, throwing my manuscript in a garbage can. I pass through a swinging doors and walk down a hallway with people walking by. I know that whatever comes next, it'll have to be done over and over, with the same disgruntled, unmotivated actors scoffing and groaning at me; and I know that I'll end up either telling the people involved in so many words that they suck or outright losing my temper and yelling at someone. It's just another average day progressing right along fine.

I burst out of the doors of the hallway and onto the next stage area. By this time of day, I'm doing things fast. I grab the manuscript and thumb through it. I take charge.

"OK, you, honey with the long brown hair, over here. It starts with you saying your line. Then we hear the music turn up and see the video of the shampoo bottle splashing through a wall of water. Then it's all of you together against that cloth backdrop right there, and you all say the same line. Then at the end it's some more video of the shampoo bottle floating through flower petals and the announcer doing a voice-over. Has everyone got their lines? Places? OK, let's roll 'em."

The model with the long, brown hair opens as the music starts.

"I don't just shampoo anymore. I rejuvenate with Vivamax."

The actors pause for the time interval of the video image showing the bottle of Vivamax shampoo splashing through a wall of water in slow motion. Then all five—the brunette, two other girls, and two guys in front of a cloth backdrop—draw their fingers through their hair, flip their heads aside, flinging their hair out, and say all together, "Rejuvenate with Vivamax."

Then the shampoo bottle is again shown, floating in slow motion, this time through flower petals as the announcer says, "New Vivamax daily shampoo with B-complex. No shampoo has as much proteins as Vivamax."

Then a chorus of singers sings at the end, "Don't just shampoo, rejuvenate with Vivamax."

The music ends, and it is over. As usual, we repeat one take after another until it starts sounding together. People steadily become more and more ornery.

I say, "I want the group to say their line louder. I can't hear you, people. C'mon, you only say one thing, it's not going to kill you to say it loud enough to hear. You, honey with the blond hair, what's your name?"

She says, "Brenda."

I say, "Brenda, darling, you're doing a darn good impression of a mouse back there. I can't hear you.

Are you shy or something?"

She says, "No, are you fat or something?"

I say, "Good one, Brenda. I tell you what, if you can call me something I haven't been called before, I'll give you $100."

I wave my arms at everyone and start up another take. After what seems like forever, I am practically yelling at the top of my lungs at people. Finally, I do my "That's a wrap," and everyone sighs with relief. I head straight for the closest doorway. Unfortunately, the camera gets in the way, and I shove it—along with the cameraman—back out of my way, saying, "Get that damn thing outta my way."

Again, the sheets of manuscript hit the garbage can. This far into the day and things start to all seem like a blur. I move from one stage area to the next through the hallways, barely aware of people around me. I'm walking through a hallway past a door that's always closed, but this time it's open. Just out of curiosity, I look in. I can't believe my eyes. It's the hugest, most beautiful office I've ever seen in my life. All the air exhales from my lungs, and I say, "Woah." It has plush carpet, expensive wooden furniture, and large paintings on the walls. There is a man sitting behind a desk who looks so regal in his flawless suit that he might have stepped out of a painting himself. He could be God. He's tall, with an all-knowing look in his eyes and perfectly formed white hair.

He stands up and says, "Come in, have a seat."

I walk in and sit in a huge cushioned chair in front of his ornate wooden desk. I say, trying not to stutter, "Wh-who are you?"

He says, "I'm a friend. I've known about you for a long time. You need me." I say, "You…you know me?"

He says, "I know you want for things to be different. I know that for years you've felt hopeless and stuck, being what you are—the icon of superficial advertisement. I can help you change things. I have that power. I can give you the change you've always been waiting for but thought impossible to happen. I can make you happy. Imagine not having to yell at people on the set. Imagine not having to work on cheap commercials. Imagine working with personable, pleasant people. Imagine doing important and interesting things."

"Wow, this all sounds incredible. I just don't know. I mean, I've been doing the same thing forever.

This is my job. Someone's gotta fill these shoes."

He says, "Take the day to think about it. Come back here at the end of the day, and we'll talk. We'll talk about anything you want to talk about. We'll talk about what you need in your life. We'll talk about your future. You've been very fortunate to meet me, and it was meant to be. Remember, I can change things for you." He lifts his arm and motions for me to go back through the door.

I get up and say, "OK, boss, uh, I guess I'll be back here at closing time. Uh, nice meeting ya."

I step out of his paradise of an office and shut the door. *Wow*, I think to myself. He can really change things for me. I can get out of this living hell vicious cycle of a life. I start walking down the hallway. Back to work.

I walk into a recording booth and immediately know this is a commercial with a prerecorded video and a yet to be recorded audio. The lines for the voice-over are in my manuscript that I pick up off a table. I'm doing the voice-over. It's a ridiculous thing that's supposed to be cute but is just plain stupid about Mr.

Pick-Up, the faster picker upper fold-away mop. A video image is taped of my face speaking, which is superimposed onto the handle of the mop. As the mop jumps out of the package, mops up across a dirty floor—leaving a clean, straight mark—wrings itself out in water, and disposes itself in a trashcan my smiling, peppy face narrates all the advantages of the Mr. Pick-Up mop. The end of the commercial fades into a chorus of singers singing, "Mr. Pick-Up, the faster picker upper for you!"

After the recording is finished, I grab the headphones from off my ears and literally throw them down on the table, saying, "God, who writes this crap?"

I stand up at the recording table and turn around. Without even opening a door or walking out down a hall, I appear on the next set, already holding papers among a chorus of singers standing in front of microphones ready to belt out a jingle for a car insurance company. By this time of day, I simply appear on one scene after the other. I am the essence of the commercial itself, the embodiment of it. I can become any part of the advertisement itself. The drums and violins break in with a peppy beat, and the chorus sings out with smiling, bright happy faces and toes tapping…

> When you're in trouble
> Out on the road
> Arco insurance helps
> You carry the load
>
> Arco insurance is
> The number one
> The least expensive
> And the most fun
>
> Call Arco insurance
> On the phone today
> The sooner you call
> The less you pay
>
> Arco insurance
> Arco insurance

After singing that about a hundred times, the chorus breaks up. I disappear out of that crowd and that room. Now I'm in a cute bumblebee costume at a long table in a cafeteria with two hundred screaming, bustling elementary school kids dressed up the same way eating bologna sandwiches and milk. Screw this! I stand up and climb onto the table. Then I start stomping the other kids' sandwiches.

"Ha-ha-ha-ha…How do you like that suckers? Carnival bologna, the one kids love to spew. Car-ni-val. Carnival bologna. You bunch of wretched larvae!"

The kids are screaming as I make my way down the length of the table, turning sandwiches into mush. Some of them throw their sandwiches and milk at my feet. The place is a madhouse with two hundred little kids in bumblebee costumes screaming at the top of their lungs. I jump off the table and bolt for a double door. I shove it open.

Then I'm down another hallway and onto another set, but I'm not stopping there. I'm going to make my way back to the huge office with the man that said he could change everything for me. It's the end of the day anyway. Nothing can stop me. I shove my way past some people without saying anything, take a pile of papers that is handed to me and throw them in the air, then I shove over a camera as the cameraman gropes for it as it hits the floor. I storm into the hall where I remember the office being and down the hallway. I turn at the door and pause for a second, gathering my wits and coming up with the right thing to say when I open the door. I reach for the doorknob, turn it, and open the door. Immediately, I gasp at what I see. The carpet, the wooden furniture, and the paintings are all gone. The huge room has been cleared out—leaving bleak, plain walls of sheet rock, a bare concrete floor, and metal brackets hanging from the ceiling. There is no desk and no regal-looking gentleman.

I cringe down to my knees and yell, "Oh, God, noooo! Oh, God. Oh, no. It was a hallucination. I dreamed it up. Oh, God. I can't take this anymore."

I feel crushed, utterly disappointed. There will be no great change for me. Somehow my mind had dreamed up the man behind the desk as I stood there earlier in the day. And there goes my hope. I have no hope. Nothing will ever save me. It will always be the same. Nothing will ever change. I'm stuck with this pseudo reality of commercial static, this living hell vicious cycle of an existence. I'll never be free.

As I stand at the top of a staircase, watching everyone find their way out of the building at the end of the day, I think of finding my way home to my cockroach-infested slum of a hotel room. I'll probably break open a bottle of hard stuff when I get home and get smashed. Someday, I think, I gotta move out of that rat's nest of a hotel room, but it's just kind of my style—misery and loneliness. Tomorrow I'll crawl out of bed and go to work to do exactly the same thing.

I've said it before, and I'll say it again. I am advertising. I've been around since before most of you were born, and I'll be around when you're gone. As long as advertisers need mindless commercials, worthless jingles, cheap catchphrases, and meaningless slogans, I'll be there pumping it out to be consumed by the masses. And you will be there with your gullible self just sucking it up, letting cheap advertising etch itself on your conscious and guide you into buying most of what you spend your money on. Like I've told you before, I don't care who you are or where you come from, my philosophy toward you is simple—just go to hell and die! I'm not a nice person.

White Wedding

It was Shari's wedding day, the most important and memorable day of her life. She was nervous with anticipation as she put the final touches into adjusting her wedding dress looking at herself in a full-length mirror. She wore an extravagant lace white wedding gown complete with trailing veils and a face veil. Her mother was repeating what she told her when she was young, that someday she knew Shari would get married. Shari was just the marrying kind. She had come this far, and now it was her big day.

As her mother tugged at the dress and she stared at her image in the mirror, Shari began to feel a déjà vu. She began to flashback in time to when she was a teenager. She remembered a hot summer night when she was sixteen. She and her friends had pulled into a gas station and were hanging out. She had just recently developed into a pretty young girl and, although still a virgin, was beginning to conceptualize her life as to what she could expect to get from men. She was pretty enough that she would be able to get whatever she wanted.

As she stood wearing cutoff jean shorts and a halter top, her butt resting on the side of the car, she visualized a sign zooming in through the air above the parking lot and hovering in front of her for her to read. It said, "SOME GUY." It zoomed out of view through the air, and she gasped and swooned. It zoomed back above the parking lot again, and she stared at it. SOME GUY. The forces that be were telling her something—that someday she would meet the guy of her dreams. It was yellow with the letters in bold face and white and frazzled around the border. It zoomed off in another direction again.

When it came back into view, it had even changed into a campy, flashing lightbulb sign with lightbulbs spelling out the letters SOME GUY and flashing lightbulbs lining out a border around the words. It hovered there in front of Shari as she stood with her butt resting against the car, full of adolescent yearning, understanding what the sign was telling her. Her friends walked up to her, coming out of the store. She snapped out of it, and the sign disappeared, but she would always remember it for the rest of her life. It was her omen that someday she would meet the man of her dreams.

And now at twenty-two, it had happened. She was getting married. For seven months, she had dated Derek. Then one night, as they walked in the park by the river, he asked her. He showed her the ring, and she became ecstatic and said yes. Then he put it on her finger. They were engaged, and they set the date for summer. Both their families and a lot of friends were given invitations. Everything went as planned.

Shari looked perfect in the mirror. She was ready to take the walk down the aisle. Her mother handed her the bouquet of flowers for her to carry and left the room to join the rest of the family in the front row of seats. Shari met her father at the beginning of the aisle and took him arm in arm. The music began playing "Here Comes the Bride." Shari and her father paced dramatically down the aisle, the enlivened faces of all the guests in the rows of seats assuring her that she looked beautiful in her extravagant wedding gown. Her father gave her away, and she stood next to Derek, in front of the minister at the altar.

The minister had the pages of a Bible opened and looked to be engrossed in the words as if he were searching for the perfect way to begin his speech. The old lady playing the organ stopped, and a silence fell over the whole crowd. Suddenly, the minister threw off his robe, revealing athletic striped cover pants and a striped jacket underneath. A thick silver chain with a bulky round medallion hung from around his neck. He produced a microphone from somewhere and held it to his mouth.

He yelled out, "All right, yall. Let's get this party started up in here!"

The band members and the old lady at the organ took to playing their instruments energetically. A heavy drum beat with loud bass guitar laid out a rhythm for the minister's rap. He rapped while waving his arms frantically to the crowd,

> Just come alive
> Yall came to jive
> Me and the crew
> To entertain you
>
> I am your emcee
> The infamous me
> Mike in my hand
> Strike up the band
>
> It's the marriage rap
> It's in your lap
> Husband and spouse
> Bringin' down the house
>
> Your hands in the air
> Like you just don't care
> We'll keep it on
> From dusk 'til dawn
>
> It's the marriage song
> We'll play it long
> Say what you mean
> Let me hear ya scream!

Then all the congregation raised their arms up and screamed. Shari stood there mortified, holding Derek's arm in one hand and her bouquet of flowers in the other. She inadvertently dropped the bouquet of flowers to the floor. She was dumbfounded about what was happening. She couldn't believe her eyes.

She uttered meekly, "Wh-what's going on?"

She looked at Derek, who was standing there acting completely normal, as if nothing out of the ordinary was happening. He suddenly broke loose from Shari's grasp and started a stomping, hand-clapping, gyrating, and spinning break dance to the beat of the music. Some of the people in the rows of seats began clapping their hands. The minister continued,

> Now Derek's down
> He ain't no clown
> He can rock the floor
> 'Til ya scream for more!

Shari stood in bewilderment, not understanding any of this. She looked around her to her father and mother sitting in the seats.

She said meekly, "Daddy? Mom?"

Everyone just seemed to act natural and not notice anything peculiar about her wedding turning into a carnival. Then the band stopped playing. Derek stopped dancing and stood back in place next to Shari, taking her arm, and the minister picked up his robe off the floor and put it back on. He picked up the Bible off the floor and looked serious once again.

He began speaking, "We've come here today to witness these two to be joined in holy matrimony. A man is said to be worth his salt when he meets the woman whom he will spend the rest of his life with and marries her."

The crowd listened, and Shari felt some relief, having things return to normal. Outside the doors of the church, gathering was a group of rowdy dogs which had jumped fences, broken leashes, and whatnot, following the scent of two females in heat. By strange coincidence, they had wound up right in front of the church. The doors to the church had been left open because of fair weather, and the two females, trying to escape the pack of wild males, ran into the church. Again the procession was completely disrupted as the pack of wild dogs ran through the church, barking and howling up a rampage.

Shari thought as she looked around, *What now?*

The sound of the dogs barking and whining drowned out the minister and caused a restless bustle among the people in the pews. The dogs were jumping onto pews, over tables, onto people, and chasing each other in a frenzy. They had spread out through the crowd. One dog bit ahold on a woman's dress and was growling and pulling it as the lady complained and tried to pull it out of the dog's mouth. Another dog was barking loudly at a crying infant as the parents tried to shoo it away. Another dog had a bite grip on the pant leg of the drummer in the band and was growling and pulling as the drummer yelled and swung at it with a drumstick. Then a dog ran up the aisle, barking, and pounced on the trailing veils of Shari's wedding gown. It got a mouthful of the lace and yanked it from side to side, growling. A man in the pews stood up and started yelling as he yanked his leg up and down, trying to get a dog that was humping his leg to loosen the grip. The dogs had taken over everywhere and were creating chaos.

The minister finally yelled to the crowd over the microphone, "Could we get some volunteers to grab these dogs and clear them out of here?"

A number of men from both sides of the rows of seating hurried around the floor, pointing and giving each other directions. Each one of the dogs was surrounded and grabbed at the collar. The dog on the drummer was pulled off; then so were the dogs on the lady's dress, the man's leg, and the one barking at the infant. The dog yanking Shari's wedding gown was surrounded and grabbed; then the wedding gown was pulled out of its mouth. After the dogs were all apprehended, two or so men held on and walked each one of them out of the front doors. The high-pitched barking trailed off as the last dog was dragged out and the two big front doors were slammed shut.

Shari turned back to face the minister, brushed Derek's arm of his tuxedo, straightened his tie, and picked up the bouquet of flowers she had dropped on the floor. She thought, *Well, now that's over*, and she wondered what could happen next. The commotions had only made her more determined to get through the ceremony.

The minister cleared his throat and resumed, "The joining of two souls, the coming together and binding of two people, the loving and bonding of man and woman in holy matrimony is what God determined to be for Derek and Shari. As we are here to celebrate their union, so is God present among us. Let me read from the Bible…"

Just then a loud machine sound resounded through the church, and all the pews felt a tremor like they had all locked into gear on a big metal brace holding them together under the floor. All the stained glass windows lining the upper walls turned into huge video screens, and the painted face of a laughing clown came on, his image showing on the multiple screens in sync from wall to wall. The lights all throughout the church dimmed, making the screens stand out brightly. The voice of the clown came out loud on the stereo system already set up for the band and the minister.

With circus-organ music playing in the background, the clown said, "Ha-ha-ha-ha! Get ready, ladies and gentlemen, for Rockin' Benches. Ha-ha-ha-ha!"

All the pew benches in the church began to rise, revealing metal legs extending from under the floor.

The people sitting rustled in their seats. The pew benches stopped rising at a height of seven feet with another metal machine sound, like a huge gear engaging. Suddenly, each row dropped back down to the floor, buffered at the bottom with air shocks in a consecutive action row after row. Each bench after dropping to the floor started rising slowly again after its drop. The people were "oohing" and "ahing" during the dropping motion as they held on to their hats. The circus-organ music played loudly, and the face of the laughing clown flashed on the video screens and moved from side to side across the screens.

It said, "Ha-ha-ha-ha! Rockin' Benches, people! Rrrrockin' Benches!"

Shari stood there dumbfounded, her marriage ceremony again turning into pandemonium. She watched in resigned silence as all the benches in the church bounced up and down with all the people laughing and waving their arms, having a ball. The pews then started doing a tilting-sideways bouncing motion whereby one side lowered to the floor as the other side rose up high and then back and forth. All the pews engaged in this motion together as the people grabbed the backs of their seats to avoid sliding sideways, yelling, laughing, and having even more fun than when they were moving up and down.

The clown announced over the stereo system, his laughing painted face flashing on the video screens, "Ha-ha-ha-ha! Tilting Benches, people! Tilting Benches! Hold on to your hats for Tilting Benches! Ha-h-ha-ha!"

Shari was becoming more upset than ever. She turned to the minister and touched the arm of his robe.

She said, "Make it all stop, Minister. Make it all stop! Can you do anything?"

The minister raised his arms to the bouncing congregation, yelling at them, "Please. Please, people.

Have you taken leave of your senses? Please, settle down."

However, no one paid attention to him. They couldn't even hear his voice over the noise level. Shari began to walk up and down the aisle with her arms raised, yelling at the top of her lungs at the people in the pews, "Stop what you're doing. This is my wedding. Make the benches stop. Someone, please, make it all stop!"

She was crying now as she tugged at people's arms sitting in the bouncing pews. She continued pleading with them, walking up and down the aisle, and eventually, the pews began slowing down; people began to become quiet; and the clown disappeared from the video screens as they turned back into stained glass windows. The pews returned to their usual still positions on the floor, the music faded out, and everyone settled down, quickly becoming completely quiet and leaving the whole church silent except for Shari's poor, weeping voice. She was crouched on the floor halfway down the aisle, sobbing. Derek walked down the aisle, held her by the shoulders, saying, "It's all right," and helped her up to her feet.

They walked back to the altar, and the minister again opened the Bible and cleared his throat, continuing, "Well, it seems we keep getting sidetracked. If everyone is settled, we'll continue with the wedding vows. Will the groom and bride please face each other. Do you, Derek, take this woman, Shari, to be your wife, to love and to cherish, to honor and to obey, in sickness and in health, 'til death do you part?"

Derek replied, "I do."

The minister continued, "Do you, Shari, take this man, Derek, to be your husband, to love and to cherish, to honor and to obey, in sickness and in health, 'til death do you part?"

Before Shari could say anything, her body suddenly flung upside down and levitated, her wedding gown hanging out to the sides all around her body. The people in the congregation said, "Ooooh," seeing her inverted. Then her levitating body floated up the aisle as she screamed, not being able to control herself. She floated to the back of the aisle and levitated there, her body slowly turning so that she could see the congregation upside down. The people in the congregation all sat looking backward in their seats at the sight of the bride in the lace wedding gown hanging upside down.

Shari screamed, "Somebody help me!"

Derek trotted down the aisle and grabbed her, turning her back right side up and helping her touch her feet back down onto the floor. Just then, the entire roof of the church blew off of the building with a horrendous wind suctioning the air inside, blowing people's hair and hats around and causing a deafening, roaring sound. The walls of the church, front, back, and both sides started falling backward very slowly at first with heavy creaking sounds. All four walls crashed to the ground outside, shattering the stained glass windows and breaking into heaps of wooden rafters, panels, and joists. Bushes blew around and were pushed down under the wreckage. Air blew over the people in the pews now exposed to the outside, and birds in trees could be heard chirping. The minister stood at the altar with the Bible in one hand, dumbfounded; and Shari stood crying, holding on to Derek.

Shari had had enough. She screamed out loud and broke loose from Derek, running over the wreckage that had stood as the doorways to the church.

To hell with this wedding, she thought as she ran down the sidewalk past the cars parked for the wedding. She kept running. She wanted to run forever. She took the veil from off her head and threw it to the side. She kicked off her shoes and left them behind. The tail of the gown still trailed behind her as she ran. She wouldn't stop. She wanted to get as far away from the wedding as possible, whatever kind of craziness had happened back there.

She was getting as far as to be in a different neighborhood, and she flagged down a taxi. She got in and told the driver to drive downtown. Anywhere but here. She didn't care about Derek, the minister, her father and mother, or any of the people who had come to the wedding, and she didn't care if she ever saw any of them again. What had happened was a nightmare, and for now she just wanted to get away. As the taxi glided down the busy avenue in the afternoon sun, she felt like she could barely believe that any of it had even happened at all. It was all so bizarre, like a movie. She was tired. She thought to herself how she would never, never again get married.

Shari left Derek, her family, and her home and moved to California. She landed a job as a waitress and also part-time work as a bit part actress. To this day, she does not communicate with her parents or any friends of hers that had been at the wedding.

Derek met another woman and married her in a normal church ceremony. He became the television game show host of *Name That Celebrity*.

Shari's father and mother never heard from their daughter again and finally arrived at the conclusion that something about the freak wedding had caused her to break communication with them.

The minister gave up his profession after the freak wedding, surrendering his robe and the Bible then hitting the highway to hitchhike across country. On the West Coast, he found a simpler way of life in a Zen Buddhist commune. He can be seen sometimes with his comrades wearing robes, handing out literature and taking donations on a street corner in the city.

The old lady that played the organ stopped describing the day of the freak wedding after people stopped believing her. The only time she talks about it is on Sunday during church at the new church when she sees one of her friends that had also been there that fateful day.

Petrification

The air. The wind. The sun. The stillness. The silence. The desert. The desert was eternal. Remaining on the surface of the planet always motionless, never changing, only becoming light during the day and dark at night, the desert existed eternally. It came before everything else and would be there after everything else had ended. It was lifeless, yet undead and vibrant. With nothing but ground and an occasional Yukta tree, nothing living existed there. The Yuktas were like cactus, preserving water from desert morning mist. This planet, Arrakhen, had many deserts on its continents, where only Yukta trees existed for miles of emptiness stretching from horizon to horizon as far as the eye could see. There was more desert than forest on Arrakhen, and since it had been discovered and colonized, not more than a minimal population had settled there in the small regions that did have rivers and forests. It was also a small planet. Those choosing to lead a life of peace if not existentialism lived on Arrakhen.

They came from all around the galaxy. Like any peaceful planet colonized by the Interstellar Federation of Planets, it had every species, every race, every language—civilized colonists representing a diverse background of planetary origin from throughout the galaxy. Those that came over the years and stayed, raising offspring and making a life for themselves, knew there wasn't much on Arrakhen. All in all, it was a dull planet. Over the years, it had been colonized by the obscure and rather destitute. The rich and elite had nothing to do with Arrakhen, although there were landowners and business owners who could be thought of as well-to-do.

Here the desert stretched on for what seemed to be forever in every direction. It was the Pharoon desert. It was bordered on the north by the Katagwa Forest wetlands; on the south it stretched all the way southwest to the coast bordering the Urama Ocean, at the southeast becoming the Hungami Forest, the city of Habab lying 490 miles to the east, and to the west the Turenge Forest and the coastal city of Uriche, 450 miles west. Nothing man-made or natural except for the desert floor, and the Yukta trees was in almost the entire expanse of the Pharoon, except for one thing: a single, two-iron runner track for land vehicles, stretching the entire distance of 940 miles between the cities of Uriche and Habab. It was built so that land vehicles could travel from city to city through the desert. Although flying in air vehicles was more popular, the Uriche-Habab land vehicle track through the barren Pharoon was used frequently. Traffic going both ways continued on it night and day, spread out over the 940-mile distance. At a spot in the middle of the desert, a vehicle would pass by about every few hours.

Way off in the distance, a vehicle began to appear. It was a small one and a slow-moving one. It slowly chugged its way over the runners of the track, creaking and sputtering. It could only muster 80 mph. Faster and larger vehicles could speed over the track through the desert at 200 mph. But this vehicle was an old one, not only small and not powerful but at present to be in disrepair. Arnes Phoneke gazed at the pulsating desert moving toward him through the vehicle's windshield. He was a do-it-yourselfer, a jack of all trades.

He owned two house/buildings in either city—one in Uriche and one in Habab. He rented out space in both of them to people and lived off of the rent. Both dwellings were frequently in need of repair, and this necessitated for him to travel in his humble vehicle back and forth on the long trek through the desert. He could not afford to buy a newer vehicle. He often thought he should sell one of the houses and not have to travel back and forth, but he could not find a buyer. Every time he traveled through the Pharoon, he knew the danger of making the trip in a vehicle that could break down at any time. He always just chanced it.

But this time, Arnes was out of luck. He happened to look back out over the track already covered, and that's when he saw it— the vehicle was leaving a trail of smoke behind it. He couldn't do anything but just keep going. However, within minutes, an unhealthy grinding sound developed from the engine. It got worse and louder; then it got terribly loud as the vehicle slowed down and came to a halt. The engine sputtered and died. Arnes cursed as he got out of the vehicle and reached to open the compartment door to the engine. He blew at the smoke forming off of the metal engine. Whatever the problem was, he was going to have to move off of the tracks and to the side while he tried to repair it.

Every land vehicle came equipped with an automatic derailleur-side motion system that picked the vehicle up off the track and moved it to the side far enough for another vehicle to pass by on the track. Vehicles operated by a system of radar. A forward sensor picked up oncoming vehicles, and the process was for both vehicles to slow to a halt, whereby one would decide to derail and let the other one pass. It also worked similarly for a faster vehicle to pass through while a slower vehicle derailed when caught up to.

Arnes Phoneke engaged his derailing system and moved his vehicle far enough to the side that others could speed by.

He got his tools out and began by removing the cover to the engine. Right away, he could see it was bad news. A pulsator rod had worn down and ground loose at its connector end. This happened to old engines, and it was a major mechanical failure that could only be repaired in a garage with a complete engine overhaul. There was no way Arnes could do any good trying to fix it with his hand tools stuck out here in the middle of the desert. The vehicle wasn't going anywhere—at least not by its own power. The logical thing for Arnes to do was rail it back onto the track and wait for a vehicle going either way to stop. If they had a towing capability, then Arnes could tow his vehicle. If not, he would have to leave it.

Arnes had traveled out from Uriche east toward Habab; however, he would settle for a ride going west back to Uriche. He did not feel like being picky. The only thing for him to do now was wait. The sun beat down unrelentingly with almost-blinding brightness. He knew that the desert heat and sun was enough to dehydrate and kill a person exposed. He thought of the large bottle of water in his vehicle. It would be enough to get him through to when another vehicle stopped. Arnes engaged the electrically driven railing/derailing system in his vehicle. It cranked and rolled steadily back onto the track. Another vehicle would be by soon; he was sure. Things would be all right.

After what seemed to be a few hours, sure enough, Arnes heard a vehicle speeding down the track and saw it off in the distance, coming from the west, from Uriche. It was a large, well-equipped one, moving fast.

As it came closer, Arnes began waving his arms and yelling out, "Over here. Stop for me."

The vehicle was traveling at 180 mph. On the vehicle there was no one at the control panel driving.

The occupants inside were all asleep on couches in the comfortable space of their luxurious rail-liner. They had not a care in the world. Why should they bother driving when it could drive itself with the radar turned on? Arnes knew something was wrong when the oncoming vehicle didn't slow down. It barreled toward him at 180 mph. Arnes screamed and jumped out of the way at the last minute. The oncoming vehicle crashed into his much smaller vehicle and scooped it into the air like it was nothing. The large vehicle didn't slow down at all but just kept on going as Arnes's vehicle busted into pieces and crashed in heaps to the side of the rail, kicking up clouds of dust. Arnes wondered what must have gone wrong and why hadn't it stopped. Arnes's vehicle was too small to trigger the radar on the large vehicle, and the force of the impact hadn't even been bad enough to wake the people sleeping inside, much less do any damage on the large one. It had just smashed through it and kept going.

A thought occurred to Arnes, and he panicked as he raced over to what was left of his vehicle lying broken in the dirt. His plastic bottle of water had been crushed, and the water spilled out. He moaned as he held up the useless, empty plastic container and thought of what he would do now. He viewed the pieces of vehicle scattered around on the ground. The biggest part of it was too heavy for him to lift or drag back over to the rail for the purpose of blocking it like before. He walked around and gathered up all the loose, broken pieces then arranged them in a pile across the rail. He looked at it and thought, *Well, that won't do much good.* A vehicle speeding by would simply barrel through it unless someone driving was alert at the windshield. Arnes knew that his only hope would be to wait and try to flag down the next vehicle by waving his arms and jumping up and down. The fact that the water bottle had been crushed was becoming eerie as Arnes became and thirstier and thirstier in the blazing sun.

After hours passed by, another vehicle came from Uriche in the west. Arnes jumped up and cheered when he saw it. It was moving at 150 mph. Inside the comfortable air-conditioned environment of this large, state-of-the-art vehicle were a man and his wife. They were arguing. He sat at the control panel in the driver position.

He said, "And you never let me explain something completely when you think I'm lying. I always have to try to make you listen, and you won't."

His wife said, "I never accuse you of lying. I respect you. I know you don't lie to me." He said, "Well, not exactly telling the truth. Or not telling the whole truth."

The two were involved with each other, and the man kept looking back at his wife sitting in a seat in the vehicle behind him so that he completely missed seeing Arnes Phoneke and his little pile of debris strewn across the track. They sped through at 150 mph, crashing through the debris as if it was nothing as Arnes jumped up and down, waving his arms and yelling "Heyyyy" at the top of his lungs.

As they sped off into the distance, Arnes moaned and started to cry a bit as he collapsed on the ground, "Oh, no. Nooooo!"

He half-heartedly picked up the debris again and arranged it in a pile back on the track. The sun was starting to bother him now as he was becoming thirstier and more dehydrated. His only option was to crouch inside of the wrecked cab that was left from his vehicle. At least it was out of the sun. There was enough room for him to prop up against a cushion comfortably. He relaxed and drifted asleep. He woke up in what seemed like a few hours later to the sound of another vehicle crashing through his pile of debris.

Disappointingly, another one had come and gone without noticing and stopping for his makeshift block. He groaned and felt like giving up. He thought to arrange the debris again but gave up. Soon it would be nightfall. He drifted to sleep again.

As the sun set over the expansive desert, Arnes slept inside of the wrecked vehicle. A biological symbiosis that was unseen and latent existed in the deserts of Arrakhen where the Yuktas grew. It had never been discovered by the sparse population over the years. A virus existed in most Yukta trees, prevalent in the fluid all throughout the trunk and appendages coexisting for the life span on the water and nutrients in it. The virus emanated from pores on the smooth, green skin of the plant at night when the pores expanded in the nighttime darkness. In this manner, the Yukta plant "breathed" at night. The viral particles could remain airborne for a few hours before dying in the air by forming a cyst when released through the pores. Light in the daytime would immediately kill the particles. The virus when inhaled into the human lungs was extremely virulent and terribly fatal. No scientist or botanist had ever become aware of the fatal virus because the Yukta only existed far into the desert, miles and miles away from where the land became forest. If anyone through the years had gotten stuck in the deep desert at night, they hadn't lived to tell about it, nor had they been discovered dead. Being in the middle of the desert at night was something no one ever did. But there was Arnes. He was soon to find out what it was like to be struck with the virus.

Arnes woke up in the morning to the early sun soon after dawn. The temperature had dropped at night, and he had become cold. Now it was already becoming hot again. He had had enough sleep but felt strangely tired. He couldn't remember ever being this thirsty. He was gasping for a drink of water. He crawled out of the wrecked vehicle, shaking as he moved. He couldn't stop shaking. His whole body felt a strange numbness, and he didn't know whether to attribute it to dehydration or some kind of stress just from being in this unusual situation. He thought now that his only chance would be to stand directly on the rail and try frantically to jump and wave his arms at approaching vehicles. Hopefully, someone would be at the driving position alert enough to see him. Arnes was beginning to consider the possibility that vehicles simply traveled too fast down the track to see something as small as his vehicle, his pile of debris, or him.

Arnes crawled back into the wrecked vehicle and positioned himself inside of it where he could see down the track either way. He would wait until a vehicle came along and run out to try and stop it.

Arnes rubbed his eyes. He was starting to have double vision. Again, he thought it was a symptom of dehydration. He did not know that the virus he had inhaled last night as he slept was beginning to multiply in his body and affect him. The virus once inhaled had gotten into the bloodstream. From there it spread through nerve tissues all over his body. Nerve tissue making up the entire nervous system and the brain was especially accommodating to the virus, having chemically what the virus thrived on. As the virus spread throughout nerve tissue and multiplied, it began to have effect on synapses and neurotransmission.

Neurotransmitting chemicals were beginning to be blocked out at the synaptic clefts. The virus was beginning to have a comprehensive effect on all the nerve tissue of the entire body, copying and replicating normal neurotransmitting impulses and creating a mock "echoing" effect of all nerve impulses. As Arnes sat still waiting for a vehicle, he did not know what was happening to him.

In a good amount of time, a vehicle appeared in the distance far down the track coming from the east out of Habab. Arnes lurched from his position and stumbled out of the vehicle. All at once, he realized there was something completely strange in the way his body was moving. He could not control himself at all. His coordination was completely frenzied. The virus had invaded his entire nervous system and was now causing for all nerve impulses to have an "echoing," repeating effect, whereby if he willed to move an arm or a leg, the motion would spread to other areas of his body and continue involuntarily. He stumbled to the ground, not being able to stand up. His whole body contorted and convulsed arbitrarily, he not being able to control the motion of it at all. He screamed in anguish,

"Aughghgh! Aughghghghgh! Nooooo! What's happening to me?"

He groveled on the ground, his body in spasms, jerking this way and that. He was too shocked and preoccupied to realize when the approaching vehicle passed by. Like the others, it was going too fast to notice him. It did not stop but simply passed by in a speeding flash. Arnes then relaxed. His body stopped convulsing, and he lay still on the ground, only his chest moving slightly in and out breathing in shallow gasps. He noticed that if he relaxed, all his muscles the uncontrollable spasms stopped. When he realized this, he became completely and ultimately consumed in a wave of sad self-pity. He could not move at all with any decent coordination, and whatever it was that had happened to him, he feared that he would not ever gain it back.

He cried out, "Nooooo! What has happened to me? What has happened?"

After having lain still for a while, he thought to move and experiment with his muscular coordination. Maybe it was only temporary after all and would soon wear off. But as Arnes willed himself to stand up, his body convulsed again every which way but how he wanted it to—the arms reverberating back and forth, the legs kicking out repetitively, and the torso gyrating uncontrollably. Again he screamed out in angst, suffering the horrifying reality of not having muscular control of his own body and feeling completely scared and helpless, alone and exposed in the blazing sun in the middle of the desert.

"Aughghghghgh! Help me! Help me!"

Of course, no one was there to answer him or help him. He had become frantic, and he was starting to feel like he was going to die there, alone and helpless. He was starting to feel terribly hot in addition to being very dehydrated, and he thought to crawl back into the wrecked vehicle to at least get out of the sun.

Convulsing and shaking in every direction, he mustered enough effort to make his body crawl across the ground and back into the vehicle's cab space, crouching and sliding under the side of it and out of the sun. He exhaled a lungful of air after the effort and relaxed. He was tired now. He thought to sleep. Maybe there was some last chance that whatever had happened to him would wear off. Maybe he just needed to sleep it off. Maybe it would go away and everything would be better, and he could pick himself up healthy again and hitch a ride on a vehicle passing by and get the hell out of the desert and never come back again. Maybe all he needed was to sleep…

But Arnes would never be well again. The virus was multiplying in him and taking over his nervous system and brain more and more. As he slept, he began to dream in a strange, bizarre manner he had never experienced before. The virus had comprehended his entire brain, and as he experienced REMs, his dream state conscious was gripped and amplified by a chemical saturation of new neurotransmitters being manufactured by the virus. He began to have the most vivid, loudest, and longest dreams he had ever had, which lasted much longer than regular dreams as in just a few seconds. His brain kept on dreaming and dreaming. His mind was locked in a chemically triggered constant dream state.

The virus was building a vastly continuing linear architecture at a microscopic level in his brain tissue.

Neurotransmission at synapses was fusing with replacement chemicals secreted by the virus, as the viral particles themselves harbored in cell after cell of nerve tissue at the nucleus, in the axon, at the tips of the dendrites, and at the synaptic clefts. Instead of normal neurotransmission, the brain tissue of Arnes's entire mind was being rewired to have a constant single transmission, which did not fire then stop for intervals but actually bridged the electric flow over synapses so that it continued steadily. Like a vast pattern connecting and sealing from cell to cell, Arnes's brain was "networking" itself into a subvert state of electric flow functioning. Similar to the multichanneled and complicated patterns of electricity flowing through silicone chips in a computer central processing unit, Arnes's brain was functioning with a lower and lower frequency. Bodily functions were beginning to be ignored as all neural activity began to consolidate in the cerebrum, cerebellum, thalamus, and brain stem. Pulse was slowing down, body temperature had cooled, and breathing was slow and shallow. Arnes's body was dying, but his mind was contained and activated by the chemical saturation of the virus.

Arnes's spinal cord and nervous system were becoming drained so that impulses would not fire through the tissue anymore. As the last impulses for heartbeat found their way through to the heart, an inert "panic" impulse kicked in and caused Arnes to become conscious one last time for a fleeting moment. He reached out with his arms, seeing nothing because his eyesight had been blinded by the brain damage of the virus. Grunting and gasping, his body jerked this way and that, and he freed himself from the wrecked vehicle and collapsed on the ground outside of it. This would be the last time his body would move. His heartbeat stopped; he stopped breathing; and all feeling and nerve transmission from his body to his brain ended. Arnes was bodily dead.

But inside his mind, a freakish physiological phenomenon was taking place. Arnes's brain activity was still occurring and regenerating with the chemical enhancement of the virus, just like a battery keeping a charge. Normal neural breakdown that would have limited any brain activity after death to thirty minutes was eliminated by the synaptic chemical frequency created by the chemicals secreted by the virus. A sustained synaptic activity was maintaining itself. The virus not only had networked a low-frequency functioning throughout all the lobes of the cerebrum, the cerebellum, the thalamus, and the brain stem whereby a continual dream state kept Arnes's conscious barely alive; it was also secreting another chemical, which would preserve the tissue inside the cranium from losing moisture and keep it from drying out.

Arnes's brain activity would be kept alive inside his cranium, allowing his conscious to remain dreaming for more than a month.

He had been dreaming steadily. He dreamed about everything—long, continuous dreams. When his body stopped functioning, somehow appropriately, he began dreaming about his childhood. He was at home again. He was seven years old playing in his grassy yard on a warm summer day with his long-forgotten brother, Alex, who was ten. They had a dog named Clover. It was a Springer Spaniel that had been named for clover-shaped brown patches on its coat. The dog barked. Arnes's mother was on the steps of the house. She turned on a hose and started spraying water on the three of them. Arnes and Alex yelled for joy as they became drenched. The dog spun off a huge mist of water from its coat. They were all so happy.

Alex chased down Arnes and tackled him onto the ground. The older boy held him down in a wrestling hold until Arnes whined out complaining.

The mother said, "Alex, don't be so rough on your brother."

Alex released him, and Arnes got up and chased him around the grassy yard. Arnes looked up to his older brother, always thinking that he himself would grow up to be just like Alex. Both of them and the dog got sprayed off with water some more and roared with laughter, running circles in the grassy yard.

Suddenly, the scene was gone, and Arnes was in the administration building in his first year of space flight school. At this point in his life, he had found out that he failed to make it to the second year of school. His grades in math and astrodynamics were not good enough, and he had scored "noncharacteristic" on the psychological profiling exams. Arnes relived one of the most disappointing moments of his life. At this time, he realized he would never pilot a spaceship.

Then he was flying through space. He began to relive his first space flight. He stood mesmerized at a spaceship window, looking at the bright, round image of his home planet as his ship soared out of orbit and away. He watched as his ship passed another planet of his solar system. It was huge and beautiful, with rings and two moons. The spaceship escaped the solar system, and the flight was on its way to the destination of another planet.

Arnes stood seeing with a brilliant periphery through the spaceship window as the ship soared through solar systems, past stars, red giants, white dwarfs, yellow giants, past planets with moons and rings, giant and red, small and black, past meteor belts with arbitrary rock masses bright as day on one side from the light of a star and dark as death on the other side. The ship soared through space past constellations, clusters of bright stars in the distance, past inert gas cloud formations expanding outward great distances, through gas clouds with the friction of the ship, causing a lit aura from combustion of the gasses, and past huge, dark, formless and nondescript rock formations the size of entire solar systems floating free in deep space.

As the ship slowed down to cruise gently through another solar system, an image of the inhabited planet showed on a monitor screen with a narrative voice giving a short history through a speaker system.

"The planet Excelcius. With postindustrial revolution technology status, the planet is in the midst of a national division shadowing the eve of war. It is similar to the Earth's history preceding World War I. The largest continent, Uripaeda, home to the largest number of industrialized nations, is the epicenter of a controversy revolving around the nation of Samiejda and surrounding nations. The fanatical leader, Horus Gaglin, gained power of Samiejda by creating the Jarchin, a movement with the objective of waging war on the other surrounding countries and ultimately the conquer and Jarchin occupation of all Uripaeda and then the entire world. Two other nations, Lechlichia and Honchya, have joined the Jarchin regime."

Arnes found himself at a great table with diplomats and leaders. He was Franascia, leader of Habsoultine, neighboring country and number one enemy of Samiejda. He was in counsel concluding that Habsoultine must be ready to defend itself as a nation if Gaglin with his fanatic Jarchin were to wage a military campaign against them. It was beginning to look as if any day this could happen. Arnes was dreaming of something he'd never done, somewhere he'd never been, and someone he'd never been. The meeting dissolved as the leaders stood up from the table.

Franascia said, "Now, gentlemen, I am going to address the nation…"

He walked to where there was a huge ornate drapery in front of a grand balcony. A steward in a black suit moved back the drapery, and Franascia stepped out onto the balcony. It was the formal prime minister's speech balcony fixated in the east side of the grandiose administrative ministry building looming three stories above the ground area of an open concrete and tile common space where crowds gathered for speeches. The crowd gathered today was nearly half a million, one of the largest gatherings of all time in lieu of the impending possibility of war. All the countrymen of Habsoultine were anxious to know what the Grand Minister Franascia planned to do about Gaglin and the fanatical Jarchin. Franascia stepped up to the banister and took a long breath as he gazed comprehensively over the vast crowd. The crowd cheered a steady cheer. Franascia positioned a microphone in front of his mouth hooked to a huge amplification system and then raised his arms to silence the crowd. He began his speech.

"Countrymen, citizens, people of Habsoultine. The time has come to unite as one, for as many, we represent nothing and are weak. As one, we are strong. As one, we are Habsoultine."

The crowd cheered.

"A madman has come of age. A madman has come into power. A madman will try to conquer the world if not stopped. We must stop Gaglin from conquering us. We must stop Gaglin from conquering the world. It seems inevitable now that Gaglin is going to claim to order the Jarchin regime, at which time Samiejda, Lechlichia, and Honchya will unite and wage war with many nations. It will happen any day now. Fellow Habsoultine, we must be ready for Gaglin's advance. I have mobilized the military. The Habsoultine Army is fortified at the Krechnian Border.

"We must stand against the force of oppression and not allow ourselves to bend. We must resist the evil and not let it overcome us. We are the rightful. The Jarchin is the wrongful. The Jarchin is the evil that will try to condemn us. Let us stand strong against Gaglin's army and let us be invincible…"

The crowd cheered emphatically for a steady, long interval.

"I am your leader. I have always been loyal to Habsoultine and the flag, as was my father and his father and his father. I love my country and will die to protect it. I will die rather than let my country fall under Jarchin control. Ask yourselves countrymen, citizens—will you die for the Habsoultine flag?"

The crowd cheered another long, steady interval. Franascia panned from left to right, taking in the vastness of his legions of countrymen. The people filled the entire common area and the intersecting streets in front of the administrative ministry building, stretching for blocks down each of the streets that existed there, packing the streets and the sidewalks. Franascia was inspiring. His countrymen believed in him and followed his leadership always. They loved him. For fifteen years, he had been prime minister. Habsoultine was a free nation enjoying the technological revolution of the postindustrial era. Franascia, as he stood with his arms raised over the throng of cheering citizens in the traditional speech balcony, was the symbol of strength and hope for these people of Habsoultine.

Arnes was dreaming of being this person, this leader, this historical power figure. He was important.

He was loved. He was needed. He would be written about in history. The half million people in front of him were his followers, his countrymen. In his real life, Arnes's only authority had been the ownership of his two humble dwellings. Arnes had never been to any planet with a country named Habsoultine; it didn't exist.

Arnes was only imagining these things in his mind as it still functioned faintly within his chemically sealed cranium. The rest of his body was beyond drying. It was shriveling up like a mummy in the intense heat from the direct rays of the desert sun. At first, rigor mortis had taken place. Then steadily, all the moisture had baked away from his exposed body like a piece of meat cooking in an oven. Arnes's near-dead corpse lay in the desert as the day turned into night and the night turned back into day for three weeks, as vehicles from Uriche and Habab sped past the scene with the wrecked vehicle and scattered debris, oblivious.

One morning, a large, state-of-the-art vehicle sped down the track toward Arnes and his area with a young man alert at the control panel. So many vehicles had passed by because most people, although it was not thought of as safe operating procedure chose to relax, sit back and let the radar watch the track for them as they talked or even slept, anything but sit at the controls watching the monotonous desert for 940 miles. However, this young man was driving his father's vehicle for the first time, taking his friends on a trip to his vacation home in Habab, and he was eager to watch the desert rushing past at 190 mph. As he sped past Arnes' scene, he just caught a glimpse of the debris, the wrecked vehicle, and Arnes's contorted body.

He said excitedly to his friends, "Hey, did you see that back there? A guy lying on the ground."

He let up on the accelerator handle and applied the brakes. When the vehicle slowed to a stop, he engaged reverse thrust, and the vehicle slowly backtracked to the area where Arnes's body lay. He braked to a stop and put the engine in idle, then shut the engine off. He and his friends were looking out the windows at Arnes and his tiny crashed vehicle. When they stopped, they thrust open the side hatch, and all jumped out, walking around the scene, investigating what remained.

One of them said, "Looks like this guy got run over."

Another one of them said, "He sure had a small vehicle. Look at this thing. It's just a tin can."

The young man who was the driver said, "This doesn't make sense. If he got hit and thrown off the track, why didn't the other vehicle stop? Unless they hit-and-ran. That's probably what happened. His vehicle is so small that it didn't trigger the radar of an oncoming. They crashed right through him and left him out here to die in the desert. He either died from the crash or died baking in the sun or a little of both. The other vehicle either hit him head on or back-ended him. After they hit him, they either stopped to look at what they'd done or just kept going. Those damn murderers. What they did was just plain kill someone. And they got away with it."

Another one of them said, "It must have happened a long time ago. Look how shriveled up he is. He looks like he's been lying out here for years, at least. Don't other people ever use this railway? I mean, doesn't it seem like someone else would have seen him lying out here for years?"

"Yeah."

One of them picked up the shriveled body, which was stiff and only weighed about fifteen pounds—the skin like a mummy; the eyes dried out, shallow, and doll-like; the teeth exposed from dried, shriveled lips; and the neck, chest, and extremities shrunken down to almost the thickness of the bone. They decided to take the body and deliver it to the proper authority once they hit Habab, but they didn't think to investigate inside his vehicle for any information as to who he was. They were all young and absentminded. They got back into their vehicle and sped east toward Habab, propping up Arnes's stiff body in a little closet space and shutting the door.

In the unseen brain activity still occurring in Arnes's mind, he was back on a spaceship soaring through space. As the ship cruised slowly outside of orbit of an inhabited planet, again a monitor showed the planet with a narrative explanation,

"Shoulsahn is a planet with vast natural resources. Colonized by the Interstellar Federation of Planets for the purpose of a natural wilderness refuge, it is enjoyed by many for its natural beauty. There are people living on Shoulsahn in private sanctuaries in harmony with their natural surroundings."

Then Arnes found himself barefooted and wearing a colorful sunning robe on a marble patio of a beautiful marble house with huge glass windows. The house was the only man-made thing to be seen for miles. It was in the middle of a vast forest covering rolling hills stretching out for hundreds of miles. Arnes could see for more than a hundred miles through the clear air.

He heard a voice from inside the house, "Are you coming in, Arnes?"

It was a beautiful woman in a colorful robe lying on a silk couch. Arnes walked back into the house. On the other side of the room was another beautiful woman in a colorful robe lying on another silk couch. A third beautiful woman walked into the room, wearing a colorful robe and carrying a glass.

She said, "Here, my dear Arnes. Your drink."

She handed the glass to him, and he took a sip. It was delicious fruit punch. The third woman put her hands on his shoulders and lowered him to sitting position on the elaborate rug he had been standing on. The two other women joined together in giving him a back massage. They all smiled, and Arnes knew they would do anything he asked them to. To Arnes's surprise, another woman appeared at the doorway of the balcony, but she was not one of the beautiful women clad in colorful robes. It was Vertice, the woman he had once been married to long ago before they had gone their separate ways.

Arnes stood up and said, "Vertice, it's you."

He walked over to her and reached out, glad to see her, but when his hands reached her, the scene dissolved. Arnes then found himself dressed in khaki clothing in a dirt road avenue lined by clay buildings of a sun-drenched city. It looked like it could have been part of Habab. Arnes did not recognize any buildings or roads. He began walking. He turned a corner and stopped, standing completely still to adjust to whom he just met. It was Salginere, the famous artist of optical illusion. Salginere had always been Arnes's favorite artist, his paintings hallucinogenic and mesmerizing in their depiction of stark, ironic fantasy, optically eluding the sense of sight with impossible geometric shapes and formless twists.

Arnes reached out his hand to him and said, "Salginere, I've always wanted to meet you. I love your work."

Salginere took his hand and said, "And I am so glad to meet you, Arnes. Come walk with me."

The two began walking up an alley and into what looked to be a bar, with people inside at tables. As they stepped in, Arnes saw that all the people were flat, two-dimensional forms who appeared visible from one side but from the other side did not appear at all. Arnes looked back to the outside sun-drenched alleyway they had walked in from, and he saw a smaller, square representation of himself and Salginere standing in the bar—inside which was a smaller square showing the same image, and inside that another, and another, and another, becoming so small that

Arnes squinted to see the miniature image that had an infinitely smaller window within each. Arnes was inside of a Salginere painting, existing within an optical illusion with the company of the artist himself.

Salginere said to Arnes as they both stood in front of the kaleidoscope-like multidimensional descending image, staring into it, "Your life was more important than you think. You were significant as all are in their own way. You were significant to yourself."

Arnes felt a warm comfort being with Salginere. He trusted him. Salginere motioned with his hand for Arnes to walk with him, and they found a door on the wall. Salginere held the doorknob and opened it.

There was a staircase stretching outward, but it was sideways, as if gravity beyond the doorway was shifted ninety degrees. The two men stepped through and turned their bodies sideways, conforming to the sideways gravity. They walked down the staircase turning at four corners. The staircase lined the walls of a square building. As they descended the staircase, they came closer not to the bottom but to the top. It was open-air with no roof or ceiling. Outside could be seen the blue sky with clouds soaring. It was incredible to look downward and see the sky underneath. They came to the last flight of the staircase and stopped. The vastness and open sense of the sky could be felt, and a breeze blew over them.

Salginere said to Arnes, "You did not die for no reason. Your death was meant to be, as is every death."

Arnes said, "What do you mean 'my death'? Are you saying that I'm dead, Salginere? I'm as alive as you are, can't you see?"

Arnes held out his hands, as if confirming that his body existed.

Salginere said, "It will make sense to you. You'll see. You have to find the rest of the way yourself."

Salginere motioned with his arm toward the wall they were standing next to, and a doorway materialized. Then he disappeared. Arnes was alone standing in front of the doorway on the staircase with the sky and clouds existing soundlessly under him, the building walls and the staircase above. He held the doorknob and opened the door. He stepped through. It was a hallway with white floor, white ceiling, and white walls, having no lights but somehow with very bright light beaming from all the white surfaces. Arnes walked through it. It was very long. At the end could be seen an opening. Arnes finally came to the end.

Again, it was the open blue sky with clouds bright and white moving slowly in one direction.

A great echoing voice sounding like it came from all directions out of the open sky said, "You are now coming to the end. For you, it was meant to be. It is your destiny. There isn't much time left. For you are coming to the end."

Arnes looked into the sky. He felt like he was being spoken to by God. He said, "Who are you? Is this God? What do you mean 'this is the end'?"

The voice continued, "You have not been seeing things the way they are. You are dreaming. You're not really standing there. You have died."

Arnes felt shocked hearing these words. Immediately, he was in denial. He said, "What do you mean? What do you mean, 'I'm dead'?"

Arnes held up his arms in front of him and looked at himself. To his complete amazement and shock, his body suddenly appeared as only a skeleton, tainted whitish bones of his arms, chest, hips, legs, and feet. Then suddenly, there was no floor beneath him, and he began to fall, rushing at great speed downward through the air.

He let out a great scream, "Aughghghghgh!"

The vehicle had arrived at Habab and the crew left it parked in its own stall at the vehicle garage, the last station stop on the long route. They carried the shrunken corpse with them as they walked home. When they arrived at the house, the young man who had been the driver changed his mind about Arnes' shrunken body. He had come to like it and decided to keep it as a memento. He would show it to people, telling them he had found a mummy in the desert.

He said, "I guess we can just keep him. Whoever ran him over isn't going to get caught. It happened too long ago anyway."

He propped up Arnes with his loose-fitting clothes in a closet and shut the door.

Arnes's brain activity was collapsing down to a small local—a volume just about an inch in diameter on both sides of his cerebrum, with a bridge in between. Synaptic functioning had finally ended in all other parts of his brain, having shrunk slowly over the great length of time his dreaming conscious had been kept alive. He was finally coming to the end where his brain would stop functioning completely and he would be all the way dead. His conscious dream would finally be over.

He was back onboard a ship again, seeing a planet through the spaceship window. As it drew closer, he saw it was a yellow desert planet. It was Arrakhen. The spaceship drew closer. Without going into orbit or stopping, Arnes was flying through the atmosphere, over the ground, over the desert. It was the Pharoon Desert. He came to the track and the scene of his wrecked vehicle. Then he was suddenly in Habab, standing in a deserted alleyway in the bright sun. He heard barking as if a number of dogs were coming closer. Suddenly, a pack of dogs appeared, running directly at him from around a corner. They were ravenous. Arnes turned to run. He turned a corner and ran down another alley at top speed, the barking following him close behind. He kept running across a street and down a sidewalk. No other person was in sight. The barking was loud as the dogs followed at his heels. Through another alleyway, Arnes fled running, out of energy and sure he would get mauled. Then he saw a doorway. Leaping for the handle, he pulled it open, jumped inside, and slammed it shut violently. The dog's barking faded away.

He could see he was in an old, deserted theater, alone. He walked into the seating area, looking over the empty seats at the movie screen. Suddenly, on the screen was an image of himself. He stared at it, and it stared back at him for a long pause. The image seemed to be alive and aware of him. He felt himself fade away, his feet no longer on the floor. Then he was the image on the movie screen staring out over the rows of seats. His other body that had been standing there was gone. He was existing inside of the movie screen. It was another dimension where there was nothingness and emptiness. He looked around himself and saw that he stood in a bleak, white void. Then the void surrounded him, shutting out the theater seat rows in front of him. The air around him was changing, rushing. One second the void was light; the next it faded to darkness. His body was fading out of view and back in. He couldn't feel himself anymore, only a numbness. He couldn't hear anything anymore, only a throbbing hum. These were Arnes's last moments. His brain activity was down to its last functioning in only a small juncture of threads of brain tissue, which was about to die out.

His last scene was in that void inside the alter dimension of that movie screen. As his sight faded in and out and finally went blank, what was left of Arnes felt a sense of ending. Relief. There was no more sound. No more feeling. No more life. His body was gone. His last sense of being was an image of himself standing straight inside that movie screen, and that's where he was frozen in eternity. His body was now completely dead. Poor Arnes the landlord. He had come and gone. His time was over, and no one would remember him. His corpse stood like a stiff mummy in that closet, where it would always be. It was lifeless. It was dried and preserved. It ended in petrification.

About the Author(s)

We the publishers decided to provide this section as a guide to this book as to who wrote it because of special and unusual circumstances surrounding the author(s). Written material was sent to us, and we published it. However, because of an explanation that was sent with the material making up the book, we were confused as to who exactly Reggie David is—if, in fact, he exists at all. The explanation itself makes the author of this book a mystery by giving a number of possibilities as to who Reggie David could be or that the name could be a number of people. In the explanation, it says clearly that the author(s) provides a number of possibilities for the reader to choose from. Why he/they wished to remain anonymous, it said:

"For reasons that don't need to be mentioned…" and so that, also, is a mystery.

One possibility in the explanation is that Reggie David is a schizophrenic man who has been homeless most of his life, since a teenager. He became mentally ill at the age of sixteen and was admitted to an adolescent mental ward in the State of Arkansas. The doctors found him to be quite intelligent and independent. He was found to have quite a mind of his own.

During a therapy session with one doctor, he declared that the doctor was the one who should be examined and asked him, "Doctor, do you ever hear any voices in your head? Really, do you hear this one?" He cupped his hands around his mouth like a megaphone and yelled directly into the doctor's ear, "Do you hear this voice in your head?"

When the doctor asked the question, "What does this mean, people who live in glass houses shouldn't throw stones?"

He replied, "That sounds like the dad talking to the kids. The rest of it is probably—wait until you get outside, then you can throw all the stones you want. Go ahead, have fun."

After being released after only two weeks of examination, Reggie David ran away from home and ended up on the streets in California.

Ever since then, because of his recurring mild schizophrenic condition—which goes away for months or years at a time but then comes back—he has been in and out of homeless shelters and on and off the streets. He traveled all over the country and experienced predominantly the beach scenes such as Key West, Miami, the rest of the Florida Coast, Galveston, Texas, Santa Monica, California, and much of Hawaii. He is a proficient surfer. In Hawaii, on the island of Maui, he was involved for about a year with a group of people who were also homeless—or "living outdoors," as they say on Maui, calling themselves members of the Church of Marijuana. They had a leader—sort of a cult-guru type— who called himself Brother Raymond, a world-traveled Vietnam veteran. Their philosophy was simple: marijuana is one of God's creations and should not be illegal. Their practice—obvious—smoking liberal amounts of high-grade marijuana at gatherings in Raymond's house called "jam sessions," in which topics of discussion led the conversation to peripheries of "higher thinking." Unfortunately, Brother Raymond was arrested by the police for growing plants in his house, which ended the Church of Marijuana, and again Reggie David moved on, leaving his beach bum surfing lifestyle on Maui.

The rest of Reggie David's life has been moving from city to city, job to job, on and off the streets. He is a drifter. His hobby is writing, and these are some of the stories he has accumulated over the years, carrying with him always a stack of notebooks in his backpack as he travels to another city, another homeless shelter, another scene. This is one possibility told about in the explanation.

Another possibility is that the name Reggie David is a pen name, male, for a writer who is actually female. She is a woman who is a mother living in a house in a very mountainous region in West Virginia. She lives in a very backward mountain community, which is deprived of modern conveniences, such as cable television. She has no telephone. The nearest store is miles down a hazardous mountain dirt road. A good amount of the food she cooks comes from hunting game in the woods surrounding her house. She herself is proficient with a rifle. She was raised in the same environment she now lives—in fact, in the same house. You could call her a hillbilly.

Her three children all moved away to the big city when they grew up, and now she lives with only her husband. These are the stories she has written in her spare time since her kids left home. She found one day that she had an active imagination and started translating it to writing. This is another possibility in the explanation.

The last possibility revealed in the explanation is Reggie David is a man who became involved in an underground cult with environmental ideals and a membership comprised of about half Apache Indians in Phoenix, Arizona. Reggie David, a writer looking for inspiration and something to write about, happened to be in Phoenix. There he wandered into a bar called the Cactus Ranch. He began drinking, and as he talked to the person sitting on the stool next to him, he found out that the bar was predominated by Native American folk belonging to the Apache tribe. There was a reservation outside the city. Looking around, he saw that they were mostly female and overweight. A few of them had braided hair with Indian handmade beads and leather lace. He found out also the bar itself was owned and run by the Apache Tribe of the reservation. At the time they were trying to pass a law in Arizona allowing for Indian-owned casinos.

As Reggie David sat and talked, he became better acquainted with the man sitting next to him. The man came around to talking about what many people who patronized the bar were well familiar with a cult, which met in places around the city made up of about half Apache Indians and half regular citizens of any kind who met other members and were invited to join. Most of the non-Indian members were people who had met someone in the Cactus Ranch. It was the unofficial bar of the cult. Reggie was given a date, time, and place to come and told there was no initiation, only a joining fee of $75.

They met in secrecy in a condemned deserted building that was once a hotel. It had a spacious lobby that the members lit up with lights run off of a generator kept in back of the building where the people parked their cars. The leader of the cult introduced himself. He was

Flying Eagle, an Apache Indian brave who—among many feats of defying death, many moons and miles of travel and gaining wisdom, and many ceremonies of mind expansion—had engaged in the Nagi Gluhapi. The Nagi Gluhapi is a ritual in which food, water, and sleep are deprived, inducing hallucination and visions, which have meaning in the brave's life. In Flying Eagle's Nagi Gluhapi, he incorporated being bitten and partially poisoned by a rattlesnake, healing during the course of his vision period.

Flying Eagle wore his traditional, tribal leather Indian clothing with eagle feathers on both shoulders.

He had painted insignia that matched the renowned symbol for mortal combat on each arm at the bicep. He said the symbols on his arms had to do with something that happened at an Indian casino in another state and refused to go into further detail. Flying Eagle then described the meaning and ideals of the cult. This was the Followers of Life Force. Their beliefs are that mankind is controlled by destiny to one day live on the moon and in deserts in technologically advanced and self-sufficient super cites, which will derive energy from solar power with the burning of fossil fuel and nuclear power made obsolete. As the bulk of the population of mankind moves to these super cities, the wilderness will be once again allowed to thrive and animals allowed to once again flourish. All the pollution, roads, cities, and man-made structures will be removed, allowing the wilderness to once again be whole worldwide as it once was before the industrial revolution. The Followers believe that a "life force" exists, which will one day make this happen.

The Followers of Life Force meet together at several locations. At most meetings, any one of many types of hallucinogenic drugs may be used as part of a ceremonial mind expansion. Flying Eagle is an expert on mind-altering substances. He often supplies very high-grade psilocybin mushrooms, including red dot amanitas and peyote cactus, which he harvests from remote areas of the desert only he knows about, making a liquid mescaline substance for group hallucinogenic effect. In many types of group ceremonies, mind-expanding drugs are used liberally by people sitting in circles.

The followers have many types of meditative ceremonies and strange beliefs. In one ceremony, the group induces one of the hallucinogens and meditates as one transcending into a telepathic trance, whereby all are reading each other's minds, becoming one collective mind. A "life force" energy something like radio waves allows them to "reach out" and read minds of people anywhere in the world. They prefer to achieve a telepathic connection with famous, significant people; however, there must be some type of stressful situation involving the person for it to be possible to "find" them mentally. They must be "projecting" some type of distress for them to stick out in the psychic realm.

For example, a Follower's group meditated and "reached out" to John D. Delorean when he was jailed for a brief time during his trial involving cocaine trafficking in the eighties. He was stressed, not knowing if he were facing years in prison. The group saw into his mind, and Delorean, unaware he was communicating clairvoyantly with a group of cult members, mulled over in his mind the construction and operation of a turbine engine. Everyone in the group sat back and learned how a jet plane turbine engine worked, seeing it inside and out, rotated, taken apart, put back together, and operated with counter-rotating fans, high-speed rpms, and turbo exhaust. It was very informative, like a technical film being shown on a screen in front of a class in a lecture hall. Years later was another interesting group session when Princess Diana died in a car crash and the Queen of England was distressed, sending out an obvious "pulse" to be picked up by the group. In her mind, she was mulling over years of paparazzi printing all kinds of things about her and the royal family in tabloids. It seemed that she was feeling defensive after the princess was killed and remembering all the years of hounding by the press. The members of the group could see memory after memory of images of the queen and the princess with extraordinary things being told about them, like watching a documentary.

Flying Eagle is a muscle-bound, athletic man in his thirties. He is an impressive figure and commands a mystic about him. He is the "wise one" and the originator of much of the beliefs upheld by the group.

Another belief/philosophy that the group believes concerns the origin of life forms as in all living organisms. It goes like this: the soul of any living thing is a mere point that moves through the body at the speed of light, in vertebrates creating patterns in the central nervous system and the mind. Mathematicians argue that a point, infinitely small, has either one or zero dimension. Therefore, a soul—dimensionless and weightless—can come from anywhere in the universe, traversing great distances to inhabit the physical body of an organism at birth. At death, as the last synaptic activity occurs in the body and the mind, the pattern created by the point collapses and simplifies down to nothing, but the point at which time the point, the original soul, vanishes from the body. Once freed, it is again weightless and can travel anywhere in the universe, again. It may also fly in to inhabit another living body under conception—reincarnation.

Imagine the area of the exact point of contact of the genetic information from the sperm as it touches the DNA inside the egg in the creation of a human zygote. The enzyme reaction of the egg's outer covering seals, and the DNA from the head of the sperm leaks out slowly to the formation of DNA within the egg. In that exact microsecond, when the two touch, at that exact area of matter, is when and where the point which is the living soul enters the living mass to inhabit it throughout its development and, ultimately, the entire life span. At a microscopic level, the three-dimensional area of matter at which the two materials touch is expansive enough for actually an infinite number of souls to enter and sometimes two or more souls enter it to inhabit the body consensually during the lifespan. This explains people who have always felt they have a "ghost," or someone living inside them.

The Followers of Life Force believe that a technological revolution will take place in the future, which will cause their great change in civilization leading to the construction of super cities and replenishing of the wilderness. It will be called the Science of Force and have to do with force beams. It will have a basic mathematical formula, which will look something like this: $F=MC>$ where the *M* stands for *mass*, the *C* for the *speed of light*, and the arrow signifies the force beam created when the matter is manipulated with special electron bombardment. The large *F* stands for *force*.

Paramount in the science of force is the slowing, stopping, and dislocation of valence shell electrons of atoms by microscopic force beams, which "catch" and direct electrons orbiting in their valence shells and thereby disrupt or create molecular bonds. Electrons flowing in patterns, originating with actual Integrated Circuit Comprehension Patterns, then amplified by Multielement Magnetic Pathways will attain physical shape, thus force beams. The beams will have the capability to manipulate electrons flowing at 14,000 mph to 15,000 mph in their atomic shells in a number of ways—one, to stop them without causing atomic explosion, thereby freeing the atom from any molecular bond. Force Beam Atomic Shaping will allow atoms to be removed from molecules, arranged as molecules, arranged in masses as shapes of machine parts and a myriad of other applications, which are now done by chemical and industrial means. Synthesized foods, medicines, chemicals, machines, clothing, building materials, and anything that is manufactured and used will by atomically formed by force beams in huge space stations, which orbit around the moon and operate off of solar power.

A new way of manipulating solar power will be part of the technological revolution. Huge floating solar cells in space will have vast amounts of flagella, which multiply behind a layer of oil moving through capillary veins in a glass surface. The purpose of the oil layer is to partially block out the sun to a usable degree for the flagella, like a pair of sunglasses. The heat energy of the oil layer provides part of the electricity and the multiplying flagella will be exploited by gathering the electric value of the adenosine triphosphate involved in the cell. In other words, the flagella will be dissolved and the ATP gathered up.

With force beams, the construction of machines great and small will be simplified. Many machines will be "formed" near whole so that bolting together piece by piece is obsolete. The construction of great buildings in super cities will be done with beams directed by great generators pointed from space and from the ground with huge dust clouds of matter incorporating into walls reinforced by metal veins also beam-formed. Great cities in the desert will be able to gather water from atomic separation of molecules, making them self-sufficient.

One can imagine how the field of medicine will advance with instruments that can direct force beams into the body and, for instance, destroy cancer cells. New medicines formed with Force Beam Atomic Shaping will advance medicinal capability. Scientists have believed in Life Force since Atlantis was cast into the depths of the ocean when the scientists involved learned how to manipulate Life Force. Scientists throughout history have believed in unknown forces that control the earth's magnetism and turning as well as life within the human body and the bodies of all living things. The Followers of Life Force with the guidance of Flying Eagle believe these changes will one day come and greatly change civilization.

We the publishers conclude that Reggie David is, in fact, one of the possibilities written about in the explanation, or even actually a number of the members of the Followers cult itself. We reason that this is a possibility because it does mention in the explanation that the name Reggie David may stand for a number of people. It stands out that the part about the cult is lengthy in contrast with the short explanations of the schizophrenic man and the hillbilly mother. Either there really is a cult named the Followers of Life Force in Phoenix, Arizona, or there is no such thing at all; and it, like the explanation itself, was made up for a strange reason not revealed. It seems feasible that the cult, if it does exist, may have a few writers among them and in addition to their meditative sessions have meetings where they discuss abstract story plots. In fact, this may be the most likely scenario: cult members being creative came up with several pieces of writing and decided to include an explanation that would list several options for the reader to believe in as to who the author was—in which case there is no Reggie David and the man who met a cult member in the Cactus Ranch is also fictional. Whoever Reggie David may be, we the publisher again reiterate that the reason the explanation was made is completely the knowledge of whoever wrote this book and in no way was revealed to us. It seems they simply wish to keep it a mystery.

The Edge

He was alone. He was always alone. He lived alone on a tropical island far out in the ocean. He had never been anywhere else. He had never seen anyone else. He had never spoken. He did not ever speak, nor did he know a word of spoken language. He had never worn clothes. He kept a small cloth-like covering made of tree leaf fiber around his waist. On the island, it was always warm, and he was never cold.

Regardless of his remote isolation, he stayed healthy. He swam and played in the warm water. When the waves got big, he swam in them, floating high up and dropping swiftly down with the twenty-feet-high swells, careful not to get caught in the crest and thrown about in the foam. He had learned long ago how to time swimming in the surf so as to avoid "wiping out" in a crashing wave and being held under, although with nothing to propel him, he could never "catch" or "ride" a wave as in surf. He was unaware there was such a thing as a surfboard or the sport of surfing. He was unaware there was anything such as civilization itself. He had never seen anything—only his ocean and his island.

There were birds that flew in the trees. Whenever he would see them, he would watch them intently, landing in the trees in groups and calling to each other.

He would yell out to them, trying to get their attention by imitating them, "Yeeeeeah! Yeeeeeah!

Cawwwww, cawww!"

He believed that when he yelled at the birds, it meant something to them, that they and he were speaking a bird language. He believed that when the birds came and landed, they were looking for him, to talk to and find out the latest news.

He would yell, "Keeeyaww, keeeyawww!" telling them how he had swam in twenty-foot waves the day before.

They would answer back, "Caw, caw!" bustling in the trees with each other until flying away.

He ate the fruit off of the trees, fruits of all kinds. He knew exactly how to tell if one was ripe. He knew exactly where all the best trees were all over the island. There was always plenty, and most of it fell to the ground and rotted. The island was the size that it would take about ten days walking from sunrise to sunset to get from one shore to the other side traversing the whole diameter. There were many small beaches, several parts of shoreline with rocky coast, and several parts with cliffs standing up against the pounding waves. He knew precisely each part of the shore. He sometimes jumped off the cliffs at places where the water was deep enough and the rock face was vertical enough to allow for a drop, or he would jump into ebb and flow pools that filled up deep enough with an element of timing.

He drank clear, cool fresh water from a spring-fed small creek. It began in the small mountain in the middle of the island with cool underground springs that always trickled steadily out of cracks in rock surfaces. He knew every inch of the entire island, practically down to each single tree. When it began to rain, he would hurry into one of several small caves, depending on his position on the island at the time. He slept at night in the warm air on one of several comfortable beds made of wrapped up leaves, also depending on his position on the island when nightfall came and he became tired.

Whenever he was in the water and saw a fish, he would become excited and try to catch it. The invention of a spear had never occurred to him, and he never could catch one. But that didn't stop him from creating a frenzy and chasing after one every time he saw it, yelling at the top of his lungs as he splashed in the water, "Ooooha! Haaaaooo!"

It had also never occurred to him to rub sticks together or by whatever means to try and start a fire. There had never been a fire anywhere. He did not know what it was. He didn't need it for anything he did during his daily routine. His usual day was very, very simple: wake up, walk, eat fruit, swim, jump cliffs, talk to birds, walk, wander about, eat fruit, sleep. He had never seen a fire. The only evidence of a fire he had ever seen was a tree that had been split in half and singed during a storm by a bolt of lightning. It had been on fire for a while then had died out in the rain. He was wandering through the forest after the storm and happened upon the struck tree. The blackness of the ash surface of the tree immediately made him gasp. He stood awestruck looking at the burned, cracked tree trunk fallen on the ground. He had never seen anything like it. It scared him. When something happened like seeing the burned tree, he would get in a certain morose mood. He was usually happy in his simple island sanctuary, but at times like this, he showed another side—a serious side. His mind knew there was something foreboding that existed always, something eerie that would always be there, a problem that would never go away and would never be solved. When he experienced this melancholy, he would think of the edge.

At one end of the island was the edge. It was a great wall that constituted the edge of the entire world in which he lived. It stretched on forever out into the horizon, walling off the ocean in one direction—and the same in the other direction. It bordered the island for several hundred yards of forest, rising up taller than most of the trees where the level of the island came down to just above sea level from the mountain. The edge was about fifty feet tall at the water's surface, rising up high above crashing waves. It was a smooth, black surface, hard and unbending like a metal, perfectly straight and flawless. It made a geometrically perfect plane; the other side of which was nothing but sky. He could see over it when he stood up the hill. It was two body lengths thick at the top. The great empty space on the other side would light up with a dim brightness hours before the dawn. Although he could not see the surface of it on the other side, he knew it was the same unending blackness.

He did not like the edge. It made him insecure. The sight of it made him feel cold and vulnerable, as if it could one day start moving and crush everything. He avoided the edge. He avoided being at that part of the island. He almost never went there. He did not stay on the side of the mountain descending toward the edge. He always stayed where it was only in the outer periphery in the distance so he wouldn't have to look at it. On most of the island, he could avoid seeing it by being in the forest; and on some of the shore on the part of the island farthest away from the edge, it was only barely visible on the horizon of the ocean. But when he swam at the shores on the other sides of the island or jumped the cliffs, he would always have to do his best to shut it out of his mind by not looking in the direction of it. Only when he became melancholy would he make the trek across the mountain, down the slope, and through the forest to where the massive black wall stood. He would stare at it for great lengths of time, wondering why it was there and why something so different from everything else existed.

One time, there was a storm, and the wind began blowing so hard that he had to huddle against a wall for hours even though he was inside one of his caves. It frightened him and left him in a very anxious mood that lasted throughout the night. After the fierce wind let up, he spent the night in the cave, staying out of the rain. He only began to feel assured in the morning when he woke up and walked out. It was good to feel the sunshine again. During the storm, he had been scared into thinking that it might be the end of the world and the sun would never shine again. It caused him to regress into his melancholy mood, and he thought of the edge. He trekked over the mountain and perched on the slope to view it. He began to think the edge controlled things somehow. He thought maybe the edge was what caused the storm. Maybe the edge was an evil force against him. Maybe the edge would eventually kill him somehow. Maybe it would start growing so tall that it would block out the sun, making everything black. Maybe giant evil birds would fly out of the air from far down on the other side, swooping down on him as he tried to run through the trees, and kill him. Maybe another edge would come from over the horizon on the opposite side of the island, gushing all the water and waves of the ocean and pushing in the beach to restrain the island between two parallel edges, then finally both would slowly move inward to crush everything and send all the land and water falling over both edges into nothingness.

Once when the wind was blowing hard without raining, he was in the water playing in the waves. He usually liked the waves to get as big as they could—the bigger, the better. But this time, the swells got too big, and the crashing crests overpowered him, throwing him into spins and holding him underwater. He thrashed in the water with all his strength and energy, trying to swim to the shore in the churning foam. He made it onto the shore, washing up fortunately on soft sand with a great swell that gushed up further on the beach than he'd ever seen water go. He thought his fear of how the edge might be trying to kill him. He trekked over the mountain and perched on the slope.

The edge was getting huge waves crashing against it. Some were so high they were crashing water and foam against it all the way to the top. Then suddenly, one huge wave crashed against it, throwing the top of the crest over the top of the edge. A huge amount of water in a line shape constituting the width of the wave flew over the top and fell into the air, disappearing behind the edge and leaving foamy water spilling off the top. This gripped his attention. He was dumbfounded at the sight of it. It happened again. And again. He stood comprehending the action. It made him feel forlorn, seeing the water fall off into nothingness. He had never seen waves do this. Moreover, he had never seen anything go over the edge. The idea of something going over it had never been within his conceptualization of the edge. It opened a venue for him. If water could go over, then a bird could go over or something else. Maybe he could go over. He walked down close to the great black wall, picked up a rock, and with all his might, threw it as high as he could toward the top. It disappeared and left nothing behind it. He stood stolid as the high winds rustled the trees noisily. The rock flying over made him feel free. The authority of the edge could be defied. He raised up his arms and let out a great yell over the top of the edge, "Hyorraaayyy, yahhh!"

Sometimes, while relaxing in the sunshine or lying in one of his leaf beds at night, before he drifted to sleep he would go back into remembering. His life had always been so simple. There were only simple things to remember. He remembered how this fish and that fish got away from him. He remembered all the different-looking types of fish, big and small. He remembered swimming in big and bigger waves at different beaches around the island. He remembered many times of jumping off each of the cliffs in the bright sunshine, hearing the loud rush of air against his ears as his body descended, exploding into the water and holding his breath as he ascended twenty feet to the surface, eyes open and seeing through the clear, warm water. He remembered times of seeing the birds in the trees and telling them about his exploits in the water. One time he told the birds that if they wanted to, they could join him swimming. He said he knew all the best beaches where the waves stood up on good days. He said since they could fly, they wouldn't be scared to jump off the cliffs. He remembered the time he told the birds that he would show them where some of his favorite fruit trees were if they got hungry and needed it. He mentioned there was plenty for all of them.

He remembered all of the bad storms that had blown the trees back and forth violently. He remembered hiding in the caves to wait out the rain. He remembered where each of his favorite fruit trees were, which ones had big pieces of fruit ripening on the branches and which ones he would walk to the next day to eat from. He remembered his only work—gathering new leaves for his beds—and the thought of doing the chore. Sometimes he would go deeper, receding back in time, concentrating as memories emerged from long ago. He would come to a point that made him feel strange. Something had been different long ago, something so long ago. His mind would shift into very long-term memory, and he would arrive at it.

Yes, that was it! He was once smaller. Long ago, his body had been smaller and weaker. He had not been able to jump and reach as far up into the fruit trees. He once could not swim as strongly in the waves. He once had been afraid to jump off the cliffs. He once long ago had not any hair on his face. At times when he remembered this, all the times he had lived and the things he had taught himself came back to him. Then he would remember something that bothered him: the edge was once not there.

Yes, it was long ago, but he would sometimes remember. The island had once been completely surrounded by the ocean long ago when he was smaller. The edge had not been there. He was an innocent boy living an innocent, happy life under the sunshine of his tropical island in the middle of the ocean. Then one day, looking out over the ocean on a windy day when the waves were high, he had noticed the dark edge behind the waves. It was very far away, and he could barely make it out. It had caught his eye, and he stared at it for a very long time. It was something unnatural. As he grew older and time passed by in a period of many, many days, the edge very slowly came closer to the island. One day it was close enough that he began to consider swimming to it. He was afraid to. He did not like it and thought it might hurt him somehow if he touched it. One day when the waves were calm, his curiosity overwhelmed him, and he swam into the water, treading water steadily and venturing further out. As he drew closer, the ominous structure became too frightening. Fear gripped him, and he lunged in the water, turning back. Swimming as fast as he could to the shore, he panted and grunted, "Hunn, hunn, hunn!"

It took him a few more trials, and finally, he overcame his fear of the huge, foreboding wall enough to get close to touch it. He drew in closer. He could see it underwater, reaching down into depths he could not swim to. He reached out his hands, his whole being alert and anxious. His voice gasped as his hands touched the surface, "Hoooo, hooooo. Aaaaah! Aaaaaa!"

He held his hands firmly against it just for a moment, feeling its monumental solidness. Then he recoiled in fear, yelling out, "Aughghghgh!"

He thrashed in the water, turned about, and swam back to shore in a panic. After that, he could swim to it without panicking and touch it. But already, he disliked the edge and found no reason to give it attention. He began to avoid that part of the island. The day came when the edge was close enough to see over it while standing on the mountain slope to the level where there would have been water on the other side. He could see there was nothing on the other side. This he would grow to hate about the edge: the nothingness on the other side.

As the days passed, he matured while the edge drew closer to the land. By the time it reached sandy beach, he had matured fully into a man. And now it had drawn the land of the island up into the forest. Since it moved so gradually, he had never grasped the conclusion of its motion—that one day it would begin to cut off the land of the island more and more. As it moved up the mountain, the level of the land would reach the top and then begin to slowly disappear over it in an avalanche motion too slow to ever be seen, except for a rare rock bouncing down the slope and over into the abyss of nothingness. He did know, of course, that it was moving inward when he bothered to remember its history. But the fact that it was slowly cutting off the land never grasped him.

One day he awoke and looked around him with a strange feeling. He did not feel as enthusiastic about swimming in the waves at the beach or jumping off the cliffs. As he got out of his leaf bed and breathed in the morning air, he felt different, as he never had before. He walked to his usual trees and ate the fruit, but something was on his conscious—a subtle message. He stood on a hill and looked out over the ocean. He had done exactly the same thing so many times before, and for the first time, he felt that the actions of his usual day were monotonous. He was moving just a little bit slower today. The climbing up the rocky hill he knew so well was just a little bit harder. Then skin on his legs, arms, and chest was just a little bit dry. He was aging.

He had come to a point in his simple life where he was looking for something different. He felt that somehow a change was going to occur for him. He wanted a change. He thought that the underlying unsolvable problem that always existed at a subtle level possibly did have a solution. He would seek the solution and feel the resolve. He would go on to live a different life after a much-awaited turning point. He thought of the edge. He hated the edge. The edge was it! The edge was what was wrong with his simple world. The edge was evil. Somehow there was something he could do about the edge. Somehow there was a way to remove it from the world. Damn its unyielding fortitude. He had to conquer the edge. He ran through the forest and trekked over the mountain then down the slope this time with unusual fervor.

He came to where the forest met the edge. He reared on his heels, gripping his fists in defiance of the massive wall, and yelled out his hatred, "Aaaaughghghgh! Aaaaaughghghgh! Yeeeaaughghgh!"

He began picking up rocks and throwing them against it with great force. The rocks crashed and broke into pieces or ricocheted off but left no mark on the wall's invincible perfection. With every rock he threw, he yelled, "Yaaaaughghgh!"

His hatred was great. His defiance was burning. *He was enraged. I hate you, Edge. I hate you. Whatever you are, I hate you. You will not haunt me until I die. Somehow I will defeat you.*

One day the clouds moved in overhead to block out the sun and darken the sky. Wind started blowing steady and hard. He made the assumption that he had time to hurry to the deepest and largest cave. The sky burst with heavy rain just as he ran into it. The wind was kicking up to a very strong force. As he sat on the ground in the cave looking out, he thought how the wind was as hard as the storm where he was forced to huddle next to the wall. This cave was better. The wind was torrential. It caused a humming and thumping sound rushing against the mouth of the cave. The trees outside were straining to one side. Leaves and branches were breaking off and flying in the wind. He was dry and comfortable in the cave. The storm beat down steadily and did not let up for a long time. He fell asleep curled on the floor and gazing out the mouth of the cave when it became dark.

It was quiet when he woke up in the morning, looking out the cave to the sunlit forest. He walked out and was immediately struck with the sight of branches torn off trees and fallen onto the ground. There was even a whole tree unearthed at the base and fallen over onto the ground. As he walked through the forest, estimating the damage, he deduced this had been the worst storm ever. The edge had caused it. This time he was sure. The edge was going to cause storm after storm and start blowing down all of the trees until the wind and rain finally caught him without enough time to escape into one of his caves; then he would be blown into the ocean and drowned. He once again began to rage against the edge. A maddened look formed in his eyes; a fierce scowl contorted in his eyebrows; and on his forehead and he bared and clenched his teeth, breathing heavily and even growling slightly. He started running in the direction to confront the edge.

He neared the wall as his anger came to a climax. He picked up a broken tree branch and, moving his arms with insane anger and strength, broke off the smaller extremities, making it into a club. Grunting like a madman, he cocked back the club with his arms, ready to strike the wall with all his strength and hatred; but then he stopped and became silent. His demeanor changed as he stood looking curiously at a sight he had never seen before. In the distance, a tree had been uprooted and fallen against the edge. He dropped the club and walked eagerly over to it. It was perfectly uprooted and leaning against the wall, the roots making up a huge clump on the ground and the length of the thick trunk bent with the weight to a gradual curve. It reached to the top with branches swaying in the wind even higher than the top.

Whenever he encountered something for the first time, he naturally took time to carefully comprehend it. It had always been beyond his ability to climb the edge, and there had never been a way to get over it.

Trees equaling its height grew a certain distance from it because of the way it shielded the sun and tree branches thick enough to climb did not reach close enough to allow for a jump to land on top of it. But now this tree had blown against it, becoming the perfect ladder. He, with his simplicity, did not grasp the concept immediately, but it slowly came into focus as he stared panning up and down the length of the tree from the roots to the top branches. He had straddled trees at the trunk up to a height where he could grab branches; that was familiar. He suddenly made the connection when he remembered how water from the tallest waves had rushed over the top of the wall. Yes, that was it! It reached to the top, and he could climb it. He could go over like he had always wanted to. It was meant to be.

He gripped the trunk with his hands and situated one foot on top of the clump of roots. The first few footholds could be taken without fully straddling the trunk with his arms. After that, he grabbed the trunk firmly with the full circular extension of his arms. He steadily moved up the trunk in small increments, clasping and unclasping a firm circular grip with his arms and also with his legs, coiling and extending at the torso. He elevated to where the trunk separated into thick branches, pulled his weight up with arm strength, and situated his feet onto surfaces in the separation, panting and slightly gasping. The hard part was over.

From there, he climbed freely closer to the top of the wall, choosing branch after branch to grip firmly.

He was becoming exhilarated, his heart pounding at an incredible rate. For the first time in his life, he was about to get to the top of it. He was to the top tree branches, and they were bending with his weight. He grabbed two at the same time with either hand and pushed against the wall with his feet. His hands reached the top, and he grabbed it with both, raising his body weight and securing an elbow. He experienced a freeing sense of excitement as he looked out into the void from this position. He hoisted the rest of his body up, planting both feet solidly on the perfectly smooth, black surface, and stood erect. He raised up both arms and cheered in victory, "Yeeeaaaaaaaahhhhhh!"

It was four or five strides in width, and he carefully stepped close to the other side with great apprehension. The empty void of nothingness and sky was impending. Now he was there at the very edge of the world.

The void was vast, seemingly even infinite, but with no visual image whatsoever for the eye to judge, scale, and distance could not be put into perspective. In fact, the void seemed limited, nonexisting.

Looking down, he could see that the other side of the edge was what he always suspected: the same perfect, smooth black surface. It reached across the world in both directions forever. It reached down into forever. Unlike the empty void, the immense black wall did give him a sense of vastness; however, it was the same simplicity—nothing more than a simple, plain black surface. As he stood like a statue with his feet near the very edge, the void filled his entire range of vision with only the wall in his lower periphery. He stood forever, comprehending it more fully than he ever had. He felt engulfed in its stillness, its looming silence reaching out in all directions where not a sound could possibly originate. He was one with its mega presence.

But it was a falseness. It was an illusion. It was an incorrectness that somehow slipped through a twilight between the sky and the earth and came to occupy the world for no reason, never to disappear and return to its origin. Somehow he felt like the edge and the void really didn't exist. They couldn't exist. They were imaginary. He had always imagined them. The edge and the void never really had existed. He was looking into what was only a dream in his mind, a formless meaninglessness, an ending to all that was material and had a meaning. It was a mass of simple shape that would disintegrate when he woke up; then he could be happy and go about his usual activity on the island. He finally turned on his feet and gazed down the top long ways, into the distance with the horizon of the ocean on one side and the void on the other.

No. It was real. It would always be there more, unmovable as a mountain. It had come from over the ocean when he was a boy and would be there always until…until…He was moved by an instinctive revelation. He realized from something like a biological clock built into him that his life would end someday, even though he had never seen another person age and die to compare himself with. He had never learned about death, but standing at the end of the world, he conceived there was an end to everything. The ocean, the island, the sun, and the edge would go on, but he would end. For the first time, he grasped a sense of time, and with that an essence of wisdom, and with that an element of authority. A concept that he could control his own destiny emerged in him. This was the change that had been waiting to come for him. This was the turning point. That unsolvable problem that had existed for so long did have a solution. The solution was here. The way to be free from the edge had come at last. The way to be free from it was to jump over it.

Wait! His mind halted as his thinking changed. He suddenly arrived at the thought he could have fallen for a trap. The edge could have put the tree there for him to climb and lured him into jumping over. Maybe when it became aware of his hatred for it after he threw rocks at it and yelled in defiance, the wall decided to kill him easily by letting him on top. His loathing for the mega structure on which he stood now made him sick to his gut. A cringe came over his face, and a definition of resolute enmity surfaced in his eyes. He stood on the structure engaged in a standoff with it, his mind made up to put an end to the conflict between them. He did not react to the urge to stomp his feet on it. No amount of yelling or rock-throwing or clubbing would ever even seem like a whisper to the unshakable giant. He would defy it even if it did mean to kill him by jumping off anyway. He would let it win. At least he would be free from it.

After that great amount of time, he turned from looking down the top of the edge lengthwise to face the forest and the mountain. It was home. He loved his island. The sun was out again, and a few birds were flying from tree to tree. He had second thoughts about jumping. The vast, empty space of the void was frightening. Maybe he shouldn't do it. Maybe he should just ignore the temptation and go back to his usual day. He thought of some ripened fruit waiting for him on a few of his favorite trees. As he gazed up the slope of the mountain, he thought again of how the edge had once not been there early in his childhood.

Then he conceptualized for the first time how its gradual motion was slowly cutting off the island and that it would start to push ground off into its void in the future. With his newfound wisdom, he felt looking out over the island that it was a small island after all, and he had discovered everything there was to know about it and searched every inch of it. Nothing new would ever be found here, and the edge would be getting worse as his life came closer to an end. It would always be there in his periphery as he stood at the shore.

Yes, he wanted to be free. He took a long, deep breath and in his heart made the final decision: he would jump. He panned the landscape for the last time, feeling a deep sadness that he was leaving home and would never see it again.

He again turned and faced back toward the void. He was brave. He was ready. He looked down, took a deep breath, bent at the knees slightly, and held his arms out. He did not yell as he let his body tilt over and fall off the edge. Immediately, he gained speed, penetrating through the atmosphere. The rushing of air cooled his body and pressurized against it with streamline force, a horrendously loud roar sounding in his ears. He reached maximum velocity, gulping for air with his mouth and cupping his hands to trap it. His eyes blinked as the cold air friction caused tears to swell and run pathways across his face. His body distanced about nine or ten body lengths from the wall. His body was not spinning but falling headfirst, downward, although the direction of down did not seem to be linked to gravity. With only the bare minimal shape of the wall, there was no object moving in position for him to have perspective to visually judge his motion. It created an optical illusion that the vast wall was down, making it the "ground" and the motion of his body across it. In other words, though he was falling, visually he seemed to be flying forward at great, steady speed while levitating a distance "above" the black surface.

He accustomed to gulping air by quick lungfuls and held out his arms, flying with his hands steering.

He seemed to fly on forever. The distance he was traveling was great. He felt wonderful. The weightlessness was exhilarating. It was even hallucinogenic: the black surface under him, the pale white expanse of the void around him, not a single object moving or rushing by, no forward or backward, no up or down, no direction at all—just a powerful force pushing at him and the constant gush of steady air, his body held in place with gravity magically removed—perfection. At one point, he conceptualized that he was not moving at all; his body was levitated in whiteness above blackness; and by queer coincidence, there was a mysterious rushing of air over his body, the gusting without origin. He could think of this, or he could remember that he was moving forward, or actually, downward. He was in flight, and it was more thrilling than any cliff jump he had ever taken. He knew he had done the right thing by jumping off. He wasn't going to be killed. He wondered if he would ever stop flying.

In time, he felt a subtle shift in the force of the air gushing against him. The decibel of the great rushing sound against his ears toned down just a hair, then steadily began decreasing as the pressure of the rushing air all over his skin began easing up. He felt the warmth of a few degrees in temperature gain on his skin surface all around his body. He began to breathe easier. He was slowing down. Still there was no way to measure his movement with only the empty, pale, and perfectly uniform whiteness of the void and the unending smooth, black perfection of the surface showing zero differentiation. Still there was nothing to be seen in any direction as the void reached out further than all sense of sight. Still there was no sense of gravity or direction, and still he maintained his distance from the wall in a flight now slowing…slowing…down.

The rush sound against his ears and the air flow against his skin decreased parabolically and stopped as his body relaxed and felt the warmth return to the skin. Then immediately, the air flow reversed and blew steadily, although much slower from the opposite direction of his feet and legs toward his upper body, agitating the hair on his legs and arms and hair on his head, which had grown accustomed to the air flow in the other direction. This motion, which again could have been mistaken for a nonmotion of the blowing of wind of no origin over the body while it levitated above the black surface, and so the guise of optical illusion lasted for another long period of time until the airflow died out altogether. He had fallen the distance downward alongside the great wall sealing off the world, and his body had traveled past the very middle of the void, reversing and floating back to rest in zero gravity again at the middle.

Silence pounded against his ears. He floated, not moving or shifting. He was not insecure or frightened. He was relaxed although slightly perplexed. It occurred to him that something would have to happen to move him; else he was stuck. He stood out like an anomaly in the vast silence of the void, experiencing the solace of being the only object in the whiteness that covered all distances in all directions except for the surface. He was like an innocent boy confronting all-powerful authority, a mouse caught in a vast space of air. His presence was out of place and insignificant like a microscopic particle, the only ever to have inhabited the void. He looked at the surface and started to ponder how to move toward it. The direction of the surface did have a slight gravitational pull, and since his path through the air had stopped, he was inching slowly toward the surface. He judged that he was moving to it. He held out his hands and arms and spread his legs, judging that he would reach it and be able to lightly hold on to the surface. His body drifted to it, and his feet, knees, abdomen, and hands felt the smooth perfection of the surface.

He did not feel unsafe or agoraphobic. He did not feel lost or that he was lacking in a foundation. He had gotten the greatest thrill flying through weightlessness, and he was still enjoying near weightlessness. He pushed ever so slightly with his hands and feet at an angle so that his body propelled across the surface as it "bounced" a small distance away from it and then floated back, pulled by the slight gravitational field. He experimented with the motion, taking longer and longer leaps. As he leaped in a wide arc against the plane, he caught sight of what looked like a line in the distance ahead. The plane did have a differentiation of its perfect blackness. It stretched on into the distances in both directions. He arc-leaped in its direction. As he came closer, he could see it was a perfectly geometric line of indented ladder steps. It reached both ways as far as he could see. He assumed the ladder steps lined the entire distance of the plane. He looked in one direction and recognized that was the direction he had fallen from. What was in the opposite direction was a mystery. He looked down the line of ladder steps going as far as he could see into the horizon of the unknown direction. He thought it was meant to be that he should find what was at the end. The ladder steps beckoned him.

He positioned himself on the line of ladder steps and thrust himself forward. He could move swiftly, catching a step with both hands and projecting himself over a number of them. He gained speed and locked into a rhythm, his body tilting so that his legs and upper body seesawed out and back as he patted the ladder steps with both hands. He moved fast over them in a straight line. He developed a determination to keep the motion up. He made a mental estimation of how far he had to go. Judging by the distance he fell, he knew he had a great distance to cover.

He wondered if it would be possible for him to pull himself the entire distance, or he would become too fatigued.

Patting the ladder steps as he floated speedily did not take much strength or energy. It was easy. He was making good distance at a steady pace. However, after a long time, the arm action was draining. He strained himself, grunting with each "throw" against every ladder step he clutched and pushed back on. After a great amount of time, he began to feel a slight gravitational pull in the direction he was coming from. His body was starting to get into a position in the void where gravity pulled down. He was out of the middle. He let his forward motion come to a stop and held on to a step with his hands and one with his feet. He rested for a while. He looked up the line of ladder steps. There was no end in sight. The line stretched on for as far as he could see. The sight of it disheartened him, making him feel like he had made no progress so far.

With a second wind, he set in motion forward again, reengaging his determination. Clutching the ladder steps and projecting himself upward became harder as the gravity steadily increased. He could not clear as many ladder steps with each clutch and push. The action took more strength. He reassured himself constantly that he was getting somewhere. At intervals, he rested, then regained his strength, and sprang forth again. He eventually came to a level that a push would only project him four or five steps. Then he started climbing two steps at a time. It was easy because he was still in lesser gravity.

He traversed more and more distance over a great deal of time with sheer determination, taking rest stops then trudging on step by step. He breathed heavily in and out. He looked up when he rested only to see the endless step ladder reaching beyond sight. The sky of the void was starting to darken slightly. The sun was going down. He now felt the full weight of his body. He knew somehow that he had to be getting somewhere. There had to be a top, or an end, or something—some kind of destination where he could stop climbing and rest his body. In time, the sky of the void darkened more. He thought it would be impossible to sleep holding the steps. He thought if he fell that he wouldn't get hurt hitting something but would again fly into the middle of the void. He grunted with determination, his mind adamant that he would not let himself fall back down. He would keep climbing no matter what.

The sky of the void turned to near pitch-black. It was difficult for him to see the indented steps right in front of his face. He had to rest more and more. All the muscles in his body were flexed to the limit and beyond. He was in agony. The thought that he would have to give up and let himself fall back down the great distance kept flashing in his mind. Still his will persevered. He had never been so determined to accomplish something in his life. After still another great amount of time seeming like forever, he looked upward. He squinted, sensing some difference in the near pitch-black dark. He could hear it. It was wind.

Wind was blowing up in the distance. That meant it was the top of the wall! His heart leaped, and he let out a loud cheer in victory, "Yeeeeaaahhh! Haaawwwwww!"

He began to be able to make out the image of the top of the wall, seeing also where the line of steps ended. He climbed the remaining distance. Even though he was in agony, he was ecstatic. He knew he had accomplished his great feat. He had done it. He gasped in great relief as he pulled the weight of his body over the top in a heap and collapsed on soft ground. Breathing heavily, he groaned and rolled over on the ground. He was too tired to contemplate that the top of the edge here was not the smooth, black surface. He got on his hands and knees and crawled a safe distance from the edge. He could make out some trees around him. It was a forest. He crawled onto a comfortable grassy patch and collapsed, falling immediately into a deep sleep.

He woke up to the sun shining in the trees and a slight, warm breeze blowing. He had made it. He had jumped and climbed to the other side of the world. A great sense of accomplishment surged in him. He stood and surveyed the edge. The edge on this side didn't stick out and form a wall. He gazed down the distance of the edge. There was no ocean here in either direction. If he was on an island, it was much larger than what he'd left at the other side of the edge. A group of birds landed in treetops, cawing. He yelled out to them, "Heee, eeyahh, hunna, na a, eeenya. Na a en a yo…"

He told the birds, "Hello. I have come from the other side of the world. You seem to live on a very big island. I'm glad to meet you. We can be friends. You are like birds I used to talk to."

He waved to them. He walked into the forest. There were the same kinds of trees as back on his island, but he saw a type of tree he never had seen before. He walked up to its trunk and felt it. It was huge, reaching up into the sky taller than he'd ever seen. He gazed through the forest, and there were many trees like this. It was the grandest forest he had ever seen. He decided to explore and hike in the direction away from the edge. He wandered into the forest going uphill.

It was a foothill. He covered a great distance and came to the top of it. He looked over the top and saw the most beautiful sight he'd ever seen in his life. He stared wide-eyed and astounded. It was miles and miles of land, stretching hundreds of miles out and up into a mountain range. It was vast, far more expansive than his island home. Land reached so far into the distance that he knew he could walk in that direction and leave the edge behind forever. Whatever he would find in this new land, whatever lay ahead on the trail of life, he would never have to see the edge again.

He turned around and looked one more time back at his nemesis, cutting off the land and opening up into the void beyond. He had solved that unsolvable problem. He had brought about the change that was meant to be. He had conquered the edge. He would walk for a great distance in the direction away from it and never come back. This was the last time he would ever look at it. Although he knew no language, he thought the universal meaning in his mind, *Goodbye*. He turned and started walking down.

Unnamed

From New England it came. It had harbored there for the summer, existing among the shuffling crowd up and down the avenue where many establishments made up the bar scene in a seaside town in Maine. It awoke at night when the sun went down and hovered above the patrons, going in and out of bar after bar. It existed where the people were loud and partying. Wherever the people were the loudest, at whichever bar the crowd was having the most fun, whatever party had the happiest people—it was there in the atmosphere, thriving off of the energy until the music and fun died down at around 2:00 AM. It especially was alive on Friday and Saturday night.

With the coming of fall, it moved south, flying in the air, blowing in the first cool front wind of the autumn. It blew into a new town with a rustling of the leaves in the trees, a chain reaction of dogs barking in their backyards, a motion of clouds through the sky and a line of cars down a crowded avenue with impatient drivers and horns honking during the rush hour traffic. No one knew of its arrival—although, as a whole, the town in some subtle way sensed it. It traveled from building to building; down street, road, and avenue; through parks and over fields—familiarizing itself with the surroundings. It was getting a sense of the town, the courtyard square, the main roads, the shopping areas, the bus station and the police station, the mall, and the hillsides of neighborhoods of houses, schools, hospitals, restaurants, and apartment buildings. It familiarized itself with the bridges, shorelines, and parks up and down the length of the river.

It took in the unusual: the "ancient" metal rafter King's Hotel sign on top of an old building, the deserted old rusty iron railway bridge over a busy avenue by the mall, the World War II tank parked as a monument with a circle of flower plants around it, the two Civil War cannon in the grass of the park around the courthouse. It experienced the usual. It hovered above the scene of crabby old Mrs. Growel shaking her cane (as usual) and yelling at a young mother at the bus stop; it saw as a hefty trucker climbed out of the cab of his truck after stalling it in the middle of the street to shake his fists and yell at a man in a car who got in his way; it saw the teenagers in their black "punk" clothes and mousse sprayed hair running through the second floor of the mall and arousing the attention of the security guard. For no reason, it focused on, and then became the mundane. It was in the hands of a woman bending over to pet her dog as it wagged its tail with the other hand holding the leash; it was the window in the donut shop with the paper sign that was faded by the sun because it had been there forever, saying, "Three for a dollar"; it was the old WCAV radio station sign that had existed on top of its building for decades since the radio station went off the air; it was the trailer at the new building construction site; a businessman's briefcase as he walked down the sidewalk after work; a car tire as it screeched rounding a corner; a deserted, old shopping cart partially submerged close to the shore in the river; a cornerstone of a concrete state building; a man's shoulder as he turned the corner on the sidewalk around a building; the rustling in some treetops in the midtown park.

It had found this new town and was getting acquainted. It was a small town. It had never been here before. It had been just about everywhere else: the West Coast, California, the beaches, LA County, San Francisco, the Northwest, Seattle, the Gulf Coast, South Padre Island, Corpus Christie, Biloxi, Mobil, Panama City, Tampa, Dallas, Houston, New Orleans, the Florida Coast, the Keys, Miami, Daytona, Saint Augustine, Atlanta, Myrtle Beach, South Carolina, the Barrier Islands of North Carolina, Cape Hatteras, the Chesapeake Bay area of Maryland, Virginia Beach, Ocean City, Washington, Baltimore, Philadelphia, Pittsburgh, Atlantic City, New Jersey, New York, Boston, and small towns all over the land of the States and New England. It moved from city to city, from town to town, from beach to beach, and from coast to coast in the free spirit of a drifter. When it got tired of a place, a circumstance, a scene, it rolled out of town like a train moving down the tracks.

When it found somewhere new, it became something new. It became something that was the essence of an entity discovered at random. It could inhabit a person's body. In one circumstance, it harbored for several years in the body of a monk in a monastery in the northeast, experiencing the serenity and solace—if not simplicity—of his religious lifestyle. It could lay dormant in a locale like a ghost or energy cloud. It once stayed harbored at the rocky and sandy bottom of a popular surfing beach in California for a summer, watching as bodies thrashed in the churning water, clutching surfboards and riding them. It once took the form of a church bell tower, existing for the frigid months of winter as blizzard snow conditions froze traffic on the streets surrounding the church before being plowed away and melting. It once harbored in a baseball stadium for the season, experiencing the swelling roar of the crowd during games. It once inhabited the body of a chauffeur for a very important corporation executive, driving here and there in the big city. For a time, it resided in a major city bus and train station, seeing crowds as they hurried to their departures and waited in lines. And one summer, it had been a roller coaster, supporting rushing cars full of screaming people.

It had existed for decades, residing in locales all across the land. It came into existence in the Golden Age of Radio, before television. In the network of power lines stretching out over a town in Midwestern America, a mixture of electromagnetic waves including all of the local radio signals, static electricity from hovering clouds and direct current in the high wires combined when lightning crashes during a storm hit the wires. The blended energy forms resulted in an original energy never discovered by science and undetectable by any means known to technology. It was in a way a form of life. It was a consciousness. It was an awareness with no color and no weight. It was a spirit with no magnetism and no electric current. It was an entity. It was the pivot, the origin, the spherical/nonspherical middle of abstract Cartesian coordinate systems containing dimensions beyond the first, second, and third. It had no dimension. It did not exist in the physical sense that it could ever be felt. It had power, although it was powerless to affect anything physical.

It was not good or evil. It did not "think" in terms of life to be defined by morals. It never affected people, changed them, or caused conflict among them. It was not a savior, demigod, icon, Samaritan, cult force, or anything grandiose. It could only communicate in a simple psychic "frequency" if and when it wanted to those who were receptive. When encountering its psychic signal, people would not become alarmed or unbelieving. They simply carried on an in-head repertoire with it, unconscious of the phenomenon of a clairaudience as if mulling over thoughts occurring naturally, generated by their own minds. In this way, it could exist in the imaginations of a number of people simultaneously. It was unseen. It had never been seen. It was unheard. It had never been heard. It was unknown. It had never been known. It had never wished to become anything with a permanent definition. It had no identity. It had never identified with any name. Within the confines of the English language whereby, God save us, everything that exists or has ever existed suffers the captivity of having a name branded to it, it existed as an entity without a name.

It remained latent for a number of days while it searched for a new situation to inhabit. It discovered the largest graveyard in town, comprised of hundreds of grave sights and numerous mausoleums situated in quaint grass covered hills with a road driveway running through it and iron gates surrounding it. It was not the oldest graveyard in the area. All the graves were dated in the 1900s. It hovered from one grave to another in the midnight hour as the wind gushed through the trees and a slight rain fell. It came upon a gravestone that read, "BUDDY FIELDS, 1934 TO 1987, WCAV LOCAL RADIO PERSONALITY. YOU'RE TUNED IN TO BUDDY IN THE MORNING."

The entity existed in a latticework of unknown electromagnetic frequencies. One frequency had the property of being able to pick up and "read" EM occurrences that are contained in a continuum, which could be called the EM continuum. The EM continuum can be considered a vast "library" of EM occurrences that happened in the past. Any EM occurrence, radio waves, nuclear explosions, lightning strikes, etc., leaves behind a signature that etches into a vast archive—a continuum which is comprised of force fields of unknown EM type existing in "extra-physical realm" dimensions, the same dimensions as the entity. One of the entity's capabilities was to be able to pick up and listen to radio and television wave transmissions of the past. It especially had an affinity for listening to radio programs of the past because itself was created from radio waves reacting with other EM phenomena.

As the entity hovered over the old radio personality's grave, it sorted through the archives of the EM continuum, scanning through the years of radio and television transmissions at incredible speed, like a thousand books with pictures being opened and "leafed" through. From the continuum emerged the WCAV *Rock'N'Roll 107 Morning Show* with Buddy Fields. The entity tuned in to the commentary just like a person tuning a dial on a radio…

"…And this is Buddy Fields, your morning 'rock' jock, your man at the wheel, your captain at the helm, livin' large and in charge. Another clear day for the Lincolnville area, sunshine, temperature in

the '60s. Traffic moving along fine on Route 81, no congestion at the Keeter Street Pass coming into town. Oh, what's this? Well, what do ya know. It's Ethel Merman. What are you doing here?"

In a completely cheesy and overly pronounced Ethel Merman impression…

"Hello, Buddy, old pal. Nice to see you again…"

"Sure, Ethel. What can I do for you?"

"I just dropped by the station to see you, Buddy. I thought I'd sing a little Jimi Hendrix if that's OK with you. Here we go…

> Purple haze, all through my brain
>
> Distinct things don't seem the same
>
> Lost my money, but I don't know why
>
> 'Scuse me, while I kiss the sky…"

"OK, Ethel. I think I've heard enough. Ethel, whoever told you, you could sing?" "Lucielle Ball."

"Ha-ha-ha, right. OK, Ethel Merman sings Jimi Hendrix, another first on WCAV Rock'N'Roll 107 radio…"

The entity remained at the grave site for the whole night until the dawn, taking in more of the Buddy Fields radio show. In fact, it stayed there for a number of days, "plugged into" the EM continuum and listening to a great number of transmissions, getting to know the humor and style of the golden radio voice of Buddy Fields. The radio show was from the late '60s. The station played rock 'n' roll and hard rock. It had been popular among a younger crowd and was the most listened to station in Lincolnville during its era. Buddy Fields had been a well-known local celebrity, appearing in public at fund-raisers and carnivals, his name sometimes being mentioned in the newspaper and an advertisement for the radio show playing on late-night television. Everyone in Lincolnville in the late '60s knew Buddy Fields. Later, in the '70s, when the format of WCAV went through a transformation into a station that played popular music including disco (to meet the listening demand of the Lincolnville area fan base), Buddy stayed on as one of the DJs. He was still on the radio in the early '80s, going back to his morning show. The station went off the air in 1983. He died a few years later of lung cancer. He probably smoked way too much.

As the entity listened to transmission after transmission of Buddy Fields, it could also see the DJ at his sound booth with the microphone fixed in front of his head and the countertop with its turntables, reel-to-reel tape decks, instrument panels and shelves of records. The visual image of the DJ was also captured in the signature of the EM continuum. The entity formed a whole, complete impression of the DJ, remembering everything the DJ said into the microphone and the music he played. The entity listened to and remembered all the jokes, the slogans of the station, the format of the program, and the style of the suave Buddy Fields. The entity had collected enough to copy the radio transmission. The entity decided it had found its identity in the small town of Lincolnville. It would become a radio station from the past and transmit a psychic radio show telepathically to a receptive audience of local citizens.

It was a brisk autumn morning with the sun creeping over the crest of the east mountainsides. The entity flew from the graveyard and hovered in among the few office buildings of the downtown area. The light-blue sun-bleached WCAV sign stood on top of an office building, the top floor of which had once been the radio station. Rusty old metal rods supported the big sign at the corner of the building top. It had once lit up bright at night with blue neon. It faced out over the downtown and could be seen over much of the area. It was a fixture, a relic from the past.

The entity flew up to the sign and roosted at the site like a bird. From this position, the entity could sense the downtown, seeing the people walk on the sidewalks and the cars drive through the streets. It was one of the tallest buildings in town and the houses of all the neighborhoods in the surrounding hills could be seen in all directions. The entity had an authority of sorts as it perched on the sign on top of the building. It began to transmit its telepathic radio show…

"…And hello out there. Buddy Fields with you on a manic Monday. Time to wake up. If you're on your way to work, grab some coffee at the Sunset Diner on Richard Street in Southside, or stop in for breakfast. Remember, they don't serve buffalo, and they've been running short on alligator, but you might get there before they run out of the hippopotamus special. You're waking up with WCAV, the Cavity, *Rock'N'Roll 107*. Janis Joplin, in the morning…

> Didn't I make you feel
> Like you were the only man
> Didn't I give you nearly everything
> That I possibly can
> Honey, you know I did"

There were about twelve people who first picked up the signal. All were in their cars driving to work. Like tuning in a regular radio signal on a dial, the radio show the entity transmitted played on in the people's minds. None of them thought the occurrence was anything out of the ordinary. They all just recognized that their own minds were thinking up a quirky radio show with a DJ Buddy Fields. They could also visualize Buddy at his DJ booth, speaking into the microphone. The audience began to grow in number, as people driving on the outskirts of town all the way to drivers out on the highway started picking up the psychic transmission of the radio show.

"…Expecting showers later on today, you can see clouds in the sky right now. This in the news: a southern California mechanic is accused of taking a gun to a car he fixed. Mr. Owen Peterson had fixed the engine of a '66 Dodge Dart several times. It kept breaking down, and the owner kept driving it back to the garage. Finally, Mr. Peterson became disgruntled and brandished a Smith and Wesson .38 Special revolver, shooting the engine in the air filter. And this, once again, proving that news isn't always pretty. You've got the rock jock Buddy Fields in the morning. You know, I'm having trouble with my doctor. The last time I went to him, I said, 'Doc, you gotta help me. I just swallowed a whole bottle of pills.' He said, 'Well, take a couple of drinks and call me in the morning.' And I'm opening up the request line here on the Cavity. If you'd like to give us a hello, or make a request, just speak up and be heard. I'd love to talk to ya. Hello, I know you're out there. You, yes, you, driving in the beige station wagon on the highway, wearing the blue knit sweater. What's your name, honey?"

A woman fitting the description realized the DJ meant her. She became excited and bashful and spoke up for herself, "Oh, me? Oh, hi. I'm Denice, hi."

The DJ said, "Denice, you're on the air. Welcome to the CAV morning show. Are you on your way to work, Denice?"

"Oh, yes."

"And where do you work?" "Sears, Roebuck and Company."

"Say, do you have any sales going on today so customers can save thousands of dollars if they buy, say, a scarf or a belt buckle?"

"Well, they can save several dollars. I don't know about thousands."

"OK, Denice. Nice talking to ya. Have yourself a fine day…And now for some trivia here on the Cavity. Our stump the press question of the day. Answer this: what are the three presidents that have buildings dedicated to them within a few miles of the White House? OK, if you can answer that, I'd love to hear from ya."

A man driving in a brown Continental on Beaver Street spoke up, "I think I got you, Buddy." The DJ said, "Good morning, welcome to the WCAV morning show. What's your name?" The man said, "Rick, I'm driving on my way to work right now."

The DJ said, "And where do you work?"

Rick said, "Interstate Security and Trust. I'm a banker."

The DJ said, "And do you have an answer to our stump the press question of the day: what three presidents have buildings dedicated to them within a few miles of the White House?"

Rick said, "I believe that's Washington, Lincoln, and Jefferson."

The DJ said, "You are correct. There's the Washington Monument, the Lincoln Memorial, and the Jefferson Memorial, and the press is once again free to print because of you, Rick. And we've got a Jefferson of our own here at the Cavity. This band was recently on American Bandstand, if you saw them. Jefferson Airplane on WCAV…

One pill makes you larger

And one pill makes you small
And the ones that
Mother gives you
Don't do anything at all
Go ask Alice
When she's ten feet tall…"

About a hundred people picked up on the message that was carrying through the air that morning as they drove and walked to work. The entity perched high on top of the building at the sign and carried on the transmission for an hour or so, looking down on the town and viewing its audience going into their buildings. WCAV was back like a golden oldie from the past. The DJ carried on…

"…Well, that's it for the morning show. We'll be back this afternoon unless someone bombs the station. Tune us in on your way home during the rush hour for news, traffic, and the best music in town. And here are the men in white, they've come to take me away. This is Buddy Fields, signing off for now. Keep reaching for the stars…"

As people filed into their workplaces, the entity faded out the show. It remained fixed into the faded blue sign during the day. In the afternoon, there began to be a trickle of people leaving work, moving on the sidewalks and driving in the streets. The entity became alert and readied itself to begin an afternoon rush-hour transmission. George Kearny left his office building through the door connecting the parking garage. He got in his '65 olive Mustang and drove out onto the street. He became amused as he remembered what he had been thinking in the morning on his way to work—some off-the-wall radio show with a comedic DJ. Just as he remembered it, again it began to happen…

"…It's the madman on the microphone, the cannibal, the omnipotent, the immortal, the one and only Buddy Fields back on the set with the turntable turning and the console on fire. I'm your voice of the media, your monster of the airwaves, piping through to your ears like smooth swede leather, following you on your drive home after the long workday. And now, that the slavery is over for today, and you are on your way to freedom, give me a buzz at the station if you've got a boss that you hate. That's right, if your supervisor, your manager, whoever you take orders from—if they are a real pain to work for, a dragon lady, a slave master, drop me a line here at the station and let's talk about it."

A young blond pretty woman in her car driving realized she was "on the line" and spoke up,

"Hi, Buddy. How are you?" The DJ said,

"Hey, out there. Where do you get the most current news and the best music?" The woman said, "Oh, WCAV *Rock'N'Roll 107*."

The DJ said, "That's right. What's your name, darling?"

The woman said, "Kari."

"So, Kari. Do you have a boss that is a real Genghis Khan, a monster, a Frankenstein?" "Yes, my boss is like those men who hold up a chair and whip the lions in the circus." "A lion tamer, is he?"

"I'm afraid of him. If I make one mistake, I'm afraid I'll get my head chewed off by him."

The DJ said, "Kari, I have what you need right here. I'm holding in my hand a bottle of Boss-X. It says right here on the label '100% effective, with no side effects.' Now the directions say, 'Take one Boss-X tablet and add it to the boss's coffee or beverage without him seeing you.' You understand the principle here, Kari. You'll never have boss problems again. That's right, listeners, Boss-X. I've got a case of it here at the station, just drop in and pick up a bottle. Here's the Mammas and the Papas on the CAV…

> All the leaves are brown
> And the sky is grey
> I went for a walk
> On a winter's day…"

People in their cars, pedestrians waiting at the bus stop, folks walking down the sidewalk, and anyone not engaged in conversation and receptive to the psychic frequency perceived it and followed it on their way home. A man in his car threw his head back and laughed at something funny Buddy Fields "kicked out"; another person alone in their car spoke out, being put "on the line" with the DJ; and a person riding in the bus nodded their head and tapped their foot to the beat of a song being played on the radio show. It continued for an hour or so, covering the rush hour. It started back up in the early morning as people did their daily commute…

"…Thanks for tuning in on a terrible Tuesday. Hey, I told ya we'd be back. No one's bombed the station yet, although we keep getting death threats. That's right, there's a serious psycho that's after everyone here at the station. The phone's ringing, lemme answer it. Oh, no! It's him, it's the guy who's been calling, saying he's going to get everyone. Say, pal. I don't know what your problem is. Just who are you anyway?" The DJ went into one of his voice impressions.

"This is Lou Costello."

"Ha-ha-ha. Oh my god! Lou Costello wants to kill us all!"

"That's right. I'm coming down to the station, and I'm gonna gun down everyone. You won't even see me coming. Say your prayers."

"Ha-ha-ha. All right then. I guess I'd better barricade the front door. Well, that's it for us, folks. Lou Costello is coming to waste everyone. In the meantime, do I have any requests? Any favorites you wanna hear?"

A man driving in a white car on the highway made a request…

"A good morning to you, Buddy, how are ya?"

The DJ answered, "Top of the morning. You're on the Express Line CAV morning show. Your name?"

"Eric."

"What can I do for you, Eric, have a request?" "*Barbara Ann* by the Beach Boys."

"All right, my man Eric. You've been served on the Express Line. Hey, you know why the Beach Boys are all screaming for Barber Anne on this song, don't you? They're being chased by Manicurist Alice.

Rock'N'Roll 107, the Cavity…

> Bob bob bob, bob Barbara Ann
> Bob bob bob, bob Barbara Ann
> Barbara Ann, take my hand
> Barbara Ann, take my hand
> You got me rockin' and a-rollin'
> Rockin' and a-reelin' Barbara Ann
> Bob bob, bob Barbara Ann…"

The entity, true to its nature, affected or bothered no one. If a person became upset with the idea of a radio station playing in their mind, they simply shrugged it off, forgot about it, and shut it out. In a way, though, the radio show beaming through the airwaves in the morning and at rush hour did control things in a subtle way. It controlled the traffic, the flow, the motion of Lincolnville. Just like the real radio station in its heyday, fans tuned it in for the music or a laugh, and Buddy Fields was to the Lincolnville surrounding area like a team of football players are to a stadium. He was the heart of the small town. There was a following of fans. They tuned in for the morning show and at rush hour on wonderful Wednesday. They tuned in for the morning show and at rush hour on thumpin' Thursday. Then it was the end of the week. A large mass of people "tuned in" to the station on their way home for the weekend…

"…I-it's more dangerous than skydiving, louder than a freight train, more fun than a roller coaster, better than a circus, it's the tower of power rush hour on 107 Rock'n'Roll, the Cavity WCAV. You've got Buddy Fields, live and in person, feet cemented to the floor, tied to the chair, and being held captive at gunpoint by Russian spies, as usual, here on a frantic Friday. Well, traffic's moving along fine, there's no accidents to report. We've got Hawkeye Henry up in the CAV Sky copter for your Friday Freeway traffic."

The voice of Hawkeye Henry came on…

"This is Hawkeye in the CAV traffic helicopter high over Route 218 going to Mariamburgh. A little congestion once you reach the Fourche Creek Bridge. Highway 109 south moving along fine. Traffic moving along both ways across the Mystic Mountain Pass, and all lanes clear after that accident earlier today on the Billings Expressway to Allendale. This is Hawkeye Henry with your Freeway traffic…"

The DJ came back, "Say, Hawkeye. You say you're looking down on Route 218, right?" "That is correct, Buddy."

"Well, not many people know this, but once you get past that Fourche Creek, on the north side, that's where the Bat Cave is…"

"I didn't know that, Bud."

"Yeah. And sometimes you can catch the Batmobile zooming out onto the highway at Batspeed. Look down there right now, Hawkeye. Tell me, can you see the Batmobile anywhere? You know, the 'Caped Crusaders.' Can you see 'em anywhere?"

"Ha-ha. I don't think so, Buddy, no." "No, you sure?"

"No, wait. Ah, yes! There they are. You were right. Sure enough, they're flying down toward Coopston, speeding through traffic. Sure enough."

"Is that them? Well, they must be on their way to fight criminals. OK, Hawkeye. Keep flying, Henry, our eye in the sky. You're flying on the Cavity, WCAV 107. Keep flying now with some Sam the Sham and the Pharaohs…

Matty told Hatty
About a thing she saw
Had two big horns
And a wooly jaw
Wooly Bully, Wooly Bully
Wooly Bully, Wooly Bully, Wooly Bully

Hatty told Matty
Let's don't take no chance
Let's not be l-seven
Come and learn to dance
Wooly Bully, Wooly Bully
Wooly Bully, Wooly Bully, Wooly Bully

Matty told Hatty
That's the thing to do
Get you someone really
To pull the wool with you
Wooly Bully, Wooly Bully
Wooly Bully, Wooly Bully, Wooly Bully.

"Well, folks we made it through to the weekend, surviving another whale of a workweek on Rock'N'Roll 107, the Cavity. Hey, some one's knockin' on the door of my booth. I'll let them in. Well, what do you know. It's our friend Harry the Hippie. How are you doing, Harry?"

The DJ went into another one of his character voices, sounding like a person stoned on drugs…"How things going, man? Wow, nice booth you got here, man. I get real vibes in here, man." "Harry, have you found a job yet?"

"Job? No, man. I don't need one."

"I see. I take it that you're not interested in a haircut either?"

"No, man. I'm one with nature, man. I let my hair grow to the length that nature meant for me, man." "What do you have to tell our audience, Harry?"

"I'd like to say peace, love, and tranquility to all, man. Stop the war. Make love, not war. Don't be more square than you have to be. Even squares can be cool, man."

"Harry, do I qualify as someone cool, or am I a square?"

"You're a square, man. But not a bad one. You're very cool for a square, Buddy. You know me. We've known each other a long time, man. I've got one for you, Buddy. Why is 6 afraid of 7?"

"Why?"

"Because 7 ate 9, man."

"All right. Nice to hear from you, Harry. Watch yourself out there. Be careful, and don't get yourself arrested, OK? Oh, don't go near the window, Harry. I don't want you thinking you can fly out of here. All right, see ya, Harry. Harry the Hippie, everyone. You can usually find him in the cow pasture after it rains searching for mushrooms. He's proof this town is big enough to have at least one hippie. I'd like to dedicate this song to Harry. Jimi Hendrix, If 6 was 9 on Rock'N'Roll 107, the Cavity…

> If the sun refused to shine
> I don't mind
> I don't mind
> If the mountains fell in the sea
> Let it be
> It ain't me
> 'Cause I got my own world to live through
> And I ain't going to copy you…

"And we're rolling home on a frantic Friday. Hello, darlin'. You in the blue Chevy, blond hair, brown shirt. What's your name, honey?"

A woman answered surprisingly, "Oh, hi, Buddy. I'm Debra."

"Debra, welcome to the *Headed for the Weekend* show here on Rock'N'Roll 107. And you are pretty, aren't you? Sophia Loren has nothing on you, honey."

"Oh, thank you." She smiled and blushed with bashfulness.

"On a scale of 1 to 10, Debra, you're a 12. How's traffic, Debra?"
"People are driving really rude on the highway."

"OK, folks, take it easy out there. You're not in the Demolition Derby. Try to make it to where you're going in one piece. Can I play a song for you, Debra?"

"Oh, let me see. 'No Satisfaction.'"

"OK, you're plugged in to the screaming freak show, the underground airwaves, the revolutionary, the cutting edge, the most anticipated, the one and only *Friday Follies* on WCAV. The Rolling Stones on Rock'N'Roll 107...

> I can't get no Satisfaction
> I can't get no Satisfaction
> 'Cause I try, and I try
> And I try, and I try
> I can't get no
> I can't get no...

"Well, I've been doing this a long time now. Maybe too many years. That's right, the last time the men in white came and took me in, the doctor asked me, 'What does this mean: "a rolling stone gathers no moss"?' I said to him, 'Well, Doc, why should a Rolling Stone gather moss when he is a multimillionaire?' That stumped him. Buddy Fields and *Friday Follies* on the Cavity. That's gonna wrap it up for now, folks.

Remember, drive safely. It looks like I'm out of here. Here come the men in white to take me away again. As always, it's been a wild time being your DJ, your man of the hour, your captain of the highway. It's not that there's a dark cloud inside of every silver lining, it's that there's a silver lining outside of every dark cloud. Until next time, keep reaching for the stars..."

The entity relaxed and ended the psychic transmission. The people were gone home, having walked down the sidewalks of the downtown, caught their last run buses, and driven their cars over the roads and highways. The sun was going down, and the temperature was dropping. It was the time of year when the leaves on all the trees had turned yellow, orange, and red. The autumn was closing in. The entity had reached out to people. It had resurrected the past. It had rested on top of the building at the faded blue sign and for one week relived the "good ole days" of remember when. And that was enough. It wouldn't stay.

Once again, wanderlust surged within the entity, and it was time to move on. A different town, a different city, a different scene, and a new experience. Maybe it would head south before winter set in. Maybe it would follow power lines out into the country, crossing over mountainsides. Maybe it would hit the coast and find another hidden island. But it would never stay in one place.

It flew around the town one more time, seeing scenes of people out having fun on their Friday evening: a group of girls laughing and walking in the parking lot outside of a grocery store, people standing outside of and walking into loud bars on the avenue of the bar scene, people and families driving in cars in the parking lot of a large movie theater. Then it became the mundane, one thing after another. It was the hands of the cashier in a convenience store; it was the huge iron clock in the face of the building looking out over the avenue in front of the mall; it was the clacking high heels of a woman arm in arm with her man on their way to a restaurant; a cornerstone of a concrete state building; a man's shoulder as he turned the corner on the sidewalk around a building, the rustling in some treetops in the midtown park. Then it was gone.

A Day in the Life

I was sitting at my usual table in Janine's coffee shop when the depression hit me for the first time. I began thinking in terms of my failures. Everything happening in my life lately was bad. I hadn't dated anyone since Karen left me. It had been four months. She had left me by her own decision. I had not wanted to break up. I guess she just got tired of me and my neurotic ways. She began to see me differently. She lost interest in my hobbies and what she at first had considered to be my qualities. The last thing she said to me was, "You're a loser," then she turned her back and walked out the door.

Maybe she was right. I've been feeling a lot like I have wasted my life. I can't help thinking I would have made a better life for myself had I chosen a different profession long ago. Maybe when I was back in college, I could have gone a completely different route and studied something scientific and logical. By now I could have been a successful computer programmer or chemist. When I'm in my apartment alone, it hits me like a "pang" of self-doubt that won't go away. I chose the wrong road in life, and now it's too late to start over.

I've been spending a lot of time alone. My friends noticed my depression. Mark Winthrop said to me something, like, "When are you gonna snap out of it, man?" I think there has been a few parties that I wasn't invited to. They are starting to isolate me. I think it's become common knowledge among the people I used to party with that I'm going through a phase, an identity crises. When I see someone that I know at the coffee shop, their complexion changes when they see me, and they...

"All right. Hold it! Hold it right there. This is goin' nowhere. Look, pal. You, the writer. Yeah, you. I can't print crap like this. I mean, what is this junk, huh? 'A Day in the Life?' This is garbage. No one will read it."

"Wh-who…who are you?

"Waddya mean, who am I? I'm the fairy godmother. I'm Tinkerbell. I'm Superman, here. I'm the book police. I'm whoever you want me to be. All you have to know is I'm in charge here. Now what I'm gettin' is you've got a real loser here. You need to spice it up 'cause I can't let it pass the way it is now. All right?"

"I-I don't understand. I'm writing my story. It's about this crisis I'm having…

"And no one wants to hear about your pitiful, little, sappy crisis, buddy. Do you understand? Now, c'mon. Start writing something people are gonna be interested in, OK? I'm giving you another chance, here. All right, back to you…"

Uh-um, OK. So I feel like I've reached a plateau. I don't know where I can go from here. The future seems to have no clarity, no resolution. There are no open doors for me. I have really bottomed out. I spend a lot of time walking in the park, alone. Sometimes I think, well, I could meet someone. Someone to talk to who is going through the same thing I am. We could help each other. But where am I going to meet this person? The city is so big. There has to be others out there on a plateau like me. It's just that it seems so unlikely I can even relate at all in the state of depression I'm in. I feel like the skin all over my body has been sprayed with 'social repellent'…

"All right. All right. Hold it! Just hold it right there. Stop everything. Mr uh, I don't know what

your name is. You're doing it again. You're doing exactly what I told you not to do. Let me put it this way: you're boring everyone to tears. I told you before I can't let something like this pass. It's just a yawn, I'm telling ya."

I-I'm sorry. All right, I guess I can make it more concise. I'll try to get to the point more, I promise.

"I'll give ya one more chance. Remember, no one wants to hear about your meaningless personal problems. You're gonna have to do something with it, something exciting. We gotta at least have a murder, ya get the picture? Something supernatural, something funny, something special. Now, if ya can't do something with it, I'm canceling you. I'm sorry to have to do this-you seem like a nice guy. But it's my job. One more chance, OK? OK, buddy. Back to you "

Ss-so. I took the train way out to the island and stood looking out over the ocean. There was no one on the beach and no one in the water at this cold temperature, for this time of year. I think I stood there for hours, just staring. I must have lost track of time because the sun started going down. I arrived at the conclusion that the ocean in winter time was like me going through my crisis: it doesn't have an end to it that can be seen. It just goes on and on as far as the eye can see and disappears into a grey haze. I feel like that's exactly where my life is: going nowhere with no distinguishing sign to show me where to begin…

"Cut! Cut! OK, that's it. It's over. That's all. You're canceled. I gave you one last chance but you blew it. You started with exactly the same garbage. I can't print useless junk like this. No one will read it. You're not a writer, you're more like a typewriter, a broken one repeating over and over the same boring thing. You need to get a life, buddy. As far as what we're doing here, I can't use ya. Get outta here. That's right, scram. Pick yourself up and vacate. I mean now! Don't make me come over there and bounce ya, you bum! There ya go, out the door. OK, that's settled. He's gone, the thing he was writing is canceled, we're doing fine. Oh, I guess I gotta deal with you now. Yes, you, reading this; 'the reader' as they call you. Let's see. OK I've got an idea. I think this will work. We're going to do a little thing, here. We're gonna pretend like this never happened, are you with me? This was never written. No sappy explanation about some guy's personal life.

No part about me canceling him. No nothing. Believe me, this is the best alternative for everyone involved. OK? You never read this. Now don't cop an attitude. Don't make me have to slap some sense into ya 'cause I will if I have to. Just be satisfied with what you've got. You're gonna be fine. No one got hurt. You'll be able to get to sleep at night and wake up in the morning and eat your cornflakes. All right, now that everything's settled you can go back to the rest of the book…"

CANCELLED

360°

"…And it's another night of basketball here on the CNBC News Network; cable television coverage by WPGC. I'd like to say welcome to the new Charlotte Center in Charlotte, North Carolina. You're listening to Pat Marnham. I'm your announcer for tonight, along with Vick Richards. 35 thousand here in attendance. Tonight's match up looks to be a real head to head shoot out between the visiting Boston Celtics and the home Charlotte Bobcats. The Celtics are at the top of the Atlantic division at this point of the season in the standings at 12 and 4. The Bobcats hold second place in the Southeast division behind the Orlando Magic and they are 10 and 6. Vick, what do you think are the key points of tonight's match up?"

"Pat, there's going to be a lot of effort by the Bobcats to stop Gary Payton, wearing the number 20 jersey. Payton scored twenty-eight points last week in the Celtics victory over the Nicks. He's hot at this point in the season. As you know, his specialty is jumpers so watch for the Bobcats double-teaming him anywhere from the twelve-foot to the fifteen-foot range to the goal, playing off of the zone defense. Payton is in the guard position, he's six feet four inches and weighs in at 180. Also in the Celtics arsenal is Paul Pierce, wearing the number 34 jersey. He's playing forward, six feet six inches, and weighs in at 230. He scored eighteen points against the Nicks last week, and he's running a 79 percentage at the foul line. He has the quickness to take it to the backboard when being defended by the likes of Bobcats' forward number 56, Brandon Hunter, or center number 24, Jason Kapono. On the other end of the court, look for shooting by number 5 guard, Eddie House, who shot for twenty-four points in the game last week against Orlando. Also look for scoring by number 22 guard, Brevin Knight, who scored twelve points in three pointers last week against the Orlando Magic."

"All right, Vick. You say that Payton, the offensive weapon of the Celtics, is the one to stop?" "That's right, Pat. Head Coach Doc Rivers has the strategy to play Payton with Raef Lafrentz, Jiri

Welsch, and Paul Pierce all at the same time so that all their shooters are in at the same time. Head coach for the Bobcats, Bernie Bickerstaff, will have the job of trying to defend against the jump shot as well as the three pointer."

"All right, Vick. And we'll be underway shortly. Again, tonight's matchup here at the new Charlotte Center in Charlotte, North Carolina, the Charlotte Bobcats host the Boston Celtics. Stay tuned…"

The players from both teams were in warm-ups at either end of the court, shooting jump shots. Fans walking through tunnels and down aisles between rows of seats were steadily making their way to their seats. Fans with body paint or wild outfits and fans holding signs were already waving their arms at cameras panning the crowd, eager to have their message or get up shown on camera. The announcers looked at statistics on papers in their hands as they talked back and forth to each other and into the microphones on the counter in front of them. Also at the long court side table were other gentlemen in suits, including the timekeeper and horn operator. One head coach knelt down and scribbled strategies on a pen board as several players knelt to study it. At the opposite side of the court, the other head coach instructed a player, holding him by the back. The player held a ball in his hand and had a towel draped over his shoulder. Fans in the corridors lined up at the many concession stands as workers in uniforms quickly served them drinks, snacks, and large plastic cups filled to the brim with beer. People made it to their seats with armfuls of food and drinks, situating themselves comfortably and passing around the concessions. Panning the circumference of the arena, the cameras showed the sections of seating in both of the two levels steadily filling up.

On the court, a player in warm-ups took an eighteen-foot jump shot. It hit the back of the rim and bounced up high, then floated down unnaturally slowly, bouncing back off the rim. The player focused closely on the basketball as it descended, his face contorting into a curious scowl.

The semilevitation of the basketball had caught his eye, but he shrugged it off, thinking he must have seen some kind of optical illusion. No one else had noticed the ball's weird motion.

Introductions for the starting five Celtics were made to a minimal reaction from the crowd. Then the lights dimmed in the arena; the theme song music played; and the arena announcer began the introductions for the five starting Bobcats. Each of them jogged in between two lines of standing Bobcats, slapped hands, and turned and waved to the crowd under the spotlight as they were introduced. The crowd cheered loudly for each of them. Then the lights came back on, and the players on both sides formed a huddle around their coach. The horn blew, signaling the two-minute warning to the opening tip-off. The starters strutted onto the court and made their way into position as the players on the sidelines sat back in their chairs. The referee held the ball in one hand and put the whistle into his mouth with the other.

He said, "Ready?" as the two players facing each other crouched, ready to spring upward. He launched the ball high into the air, and the two players leaped for it. One hand reached higher than the other and slapped the ball to a team player as the ref blew the whistle for the clock to start. Pat Marnham began the play by play...

"And the Celtics come away with it, Davis handling the ball at half court. He gives to Welsch, Bobcats going to the zone defense. Throw to Pierce, Pierce up for the jumper, an eighteen-footer. Scores! And the Celtics with the first points on the board. Hunter handles it in bounds for the Bobcats. Hunter at half court, throws to House on the perimeter, House dribbles, covered by Davis. House to Hart, Hart for the jumper, rebound, Kapono up for it along with Lafrentz, Lafrentz wins the rebound for the Celtics. Celtics with possession..."

As the game played on, some fans waited for their food and drinks at a concession stand in the main corridor. The rise and fall of the noise of the crowd could be heard in the distance. A stand attendant dressed in a bright-red shirt with a name tag and a Bobcat cap charged for the concessions on a cash register and handed over four hot dogs. Then the attendant finished filling up four beer cups to the brim and inserted them in a cardboard carryall. The attendant handed over the tray to the fan but let go of it before the fan grabbed it. To the amazement of the fan, it floated weightless in air. The fan recoiled and said, "Oh!" as the attendant and others behind the counter as well as the fans waiting in line all gawked at the tray of beers floating in the air. Someone said, "Look at that!" Another said, "Oh my god!" and they all gasped. The fan who paid reached out and grabbed the tray, pulling it into his possession.

He said, "No way. That didn't just happen."

The people all stood staring at him holding his cardboard tray of beers, talking among themselves,

"Wow, did you see that?" "I can't believe it."

"That must have been some trick, or something."

The game was progressing in the first quarter. The Celtics had pulled ahead to lead 13 to 6. Pat Marnham continued the play by play…

"Ricky Davis dribbles the ball across the half court line. He gives to Payton. Payton drives it to the paint. Short jumper. It won't go. Rebound into a crowd, they fight for possession, and the ball slapped out of bounds. The official calls Celtic possession. Davis throws it in. One-on-one coverage. He can't find a man. He launches it to Pierce as Pierce gets open beyond the three-point line. He'll shoot, Pierce from downtown… good! And Pierce scores three on his first attempt at the three pointer. Boston widening the margin to ten points, 16 to 6…"

A small number of fans at the very front of the balcony of the deck level at midcourt were standing and cheering energetically to the Bobcats. They were wearing wild red and blue mop wigs and had their faces painted red and blue. Anytime they saw a camera pan the crowd in their direction, they grabbed a sign that had a painted image of the head of a mean-looking cat with a frowning man wearing a clover hat hanging limp in the mouth of the cat and waved it up and down for the camera. Sitting directly behind them was a row of four passing a box of popcorn from one to the other. The one passing the box felt the weight of it lifted, and he released his hold on it. It floated in the air next to him as he kept his attention on the action on the court.

The man next to him saw it floating and said, "Holy cow!"

The box of popcorn rose up slowly into the air above their heads as they all gasped and stared. People sitting around started yelling and pointing, "Hey, look at that thing!"

Someone threw a balled-up paper peanuts bag at the box of popcorn, and it spilled out all over people's heads and dropped to the floor between seat rows. The fans laughed, and the zealots with the body paint looked back into the crowd, threw their arms up, and cheered at the top of their lungs, not having seen what happened with the box of popcorn. The game played on…

"…Long pass to Kapono in the paint. The big center can't get a shot at the hoop. He drops it back to House. House dribbles, maneuvers. Finds Hunter. Hunter at the three point line. He's all alone. Hunter from downtown. Swish! That's one for one at the three point for Hunter."

Outside the building, a security guard was trolleying down the sidewalk in his electric car, glancing in this direction and that he was keeping an eye out for teenagers or anyone loitering outside the building while other guards in electric cars were patrolling the parking areas guarding the huge number of parked vehicles. The guard was looking in the direction of one of the great "super" doorways of the arena when something at the base of the wall caught his eye. It looked like a line in the foundation of the building he had never noticed before. He trudged over the grass in his electric car and stopped right at the wall of the building. To his amazement, there was a gap about six inches wide in the foundation of the building right at ground level. Looking in both directions down the wall, he could see the gap covered the whole outside of the building where he stood. His first thought was the foundation of the building had cracked due to some earth tremor or something. Maybe there was some flaw in the construction. It was a new building. He got on his walkie-talkie.

"Hello, Earl. Number 41." "Watchya need, Wiley."

"Listen. Somebody's got to come down here to the east portal. The building's coming apart!" "Say again."

"You heard me. I said, the building is coming apart!"

Wiley looked closely at the gap and realized it was becoming bigger. That really shocked him.

He yelled out, "Whooaww!" and began taking steps backward. He bumped into his electric car and continued backing up as he began to comprehend physically the phenomenon he was witnessing.

He said, "It's all coming up! It's floating up!"

The voice on the walkie-talkie said, "Wiley, are you there? Ten-four."

He put the walkie-talkie to his mouth and said, "Earl, you ain't gonna believe this. The whole damn arena is coming off the ground. Earl, the arena is starting to float up in the air!"

Pat Marnham and Vick Richards traded comments during a time-out, "Vick, it looks as if the Bobcats are being outmanned by the Celtics."

"I agree, Pat. What Charlotte is lacking the most right now is a tough defense at the goal. They're not standing their ground, and they're letting Celtic players step in and make layups. You can see here on the replay with the big center Jason Kapono as Gary Payton just blows past him for 2. What Head Coach Bernie Bickerstaff needs to do is forget about playing man-to-man. He keeps switching from zone to man-to-man, from man-to-man to zone. He needs to stick with the zone, maybe put in another player off the bench with some height like Steve Smith and get some double-teaming on whoever the Celtics takes the ball down close to the goal. If he doesn't do that, the Celtics are just going to keep increasing the gap."

Pat Marnham said, "And the score with 4:32 left in the quarter Celtics 21, Bobcats 14. They come back in from the time-out. Jahidi White in for Brevin Knight on the Charlotte team, Walter McCarty takes the place of Ricky Davis for Boston. Ball in play. House with possession on the three-point perimeter, dribbles to the foul line, evades Pierce the defender on man-to-man. Throws to Kapono under the goal. He puts it up, hook shot, and he is fouled. Foul committed by number 45 Lafrentz. That's two on Lafrentz. He comes out of the game, and Doc Rivers sends in six-foot-ten Kendrick Perkins, number 43, at center, weighing in at 280. Kapono at the line. Misses. Kapono is shooting a 67 percentage in free throws. And he makes the second. Ball in bounds, crosscourt to Welsch, he dribbles as they set up. Pierce with the ball, he struggles, can't get inside. Back out to Payton, who chooses not to go for the three pointer even though no one was guarding him. Payton maneuvers at the top of the key. He has Perkins under the goal. Nothin' doin' there, Kapono all over him. Back out to Payton again, 8 showing on the shot clock. Payton at the top of the key, jumps high up with the ball and whoah, oh! Holy moly! Payton just floats in the air from the top of the key all the way to pay dirt and slam-dunks the ball! That was the most incredible move I have ever seen on a basketball court! He just seemed to fly in the air!"

The crowd resounded with a dramatic "Aaawwww," and Vick Richards said, "Oh, what an incredible leap by Payton, who seems to float across the court like Superman!"

Pat Marnham continued, "White now with the ball. He looks confused, as if that leap by Payton were illegal. Now he makes his way inside the three point. He finds Hart. Welsch on him immediately, and then McCarty, double-teamed. Hart gets rid of it, gives to Hunter at the three point. He sets, Hart from downtown. Oh! And an incredible leap by Pierce who blocks the shot at the top of its arc coming at least eight feet off the floor! What is going on here? That was a superhuman jump by Pierce!"

The crowd came to a crescendo at maximum decibel, and the entire arena stood on their feet. The players ran to the other end of the court as Boston went on the offensive.

Vick Richards said, "I do not believe what I've just seen here, Pat. Gary Payton just floated through the air, and now Paul Pierce jumps sky-high. Something very strange is going on here."

The coaches from both teams were standing at the sidelines, dumbfounded.

Pat Marnham continued, "Welsch has it, he gives to Payton. And now what! The basketball continues to rise up into the air. It won't fall! It's hanging there about fifteen feet in the air, too high to reach. Oh, this is incredible! Eddie House jumps into the air, coming ten feet off the floor, and grabs the ball. Other players fly into the air and fight for the ball. This is madness breaking out! Coach Bickerstaff calls time-out, but we have players jumping in the air and sailing high above the floor. There goes Hunter, there's Hart, McCarty takes a flying leap, Perkins launches into the air. The coaches are trying to get the players to the sideline. Oh my god! There's fans in the stands jumping out of their seats. A couple of fans leap off of the deck level.

They're sailing into the crowd in the lower level. Everywhere in the arena people are starting to jump around in less and less gravity. I feel light as a feather. I've never seen anything like this."

The arena announcer came on the loudspeaker and said, "We are having technical difficulties. Please remain in your seats. Please remain calm."

Outside a small number of people were yelling frantically and pointing at the building. It had risen in the air too slowly for people inside to feel the shift in gravity. Now it was more than two hundred feet high, floating in the air. Police cars and fire engines were pulling into the parking area with sirens blaring and lights flashing. The huge floating arena then began to rotate top over bottom.

A few people yelled out, "Look, it's starting to turn!"

Inside, more and more people were jumping into the air. Then everyone started noticing the slant of gravity as the arena began rotating and creating an angle. Many people grabbed on to their seats or whatever they could get ahold of.

Pat Marnham kept up with the commentary, speaking loudly into the microphone, "This place has gone crazy! And now I'm starting to feel a slant. Everyone can feel it. I believe this arena is turning over! People are grabbing onto railings and chairs to hold themselves down. We're almost at ninety degrees.

Loose objects are flying through the air like a rainstorm. The west side of the arena has become the floor. A player is hanging from the rim of a goal. People are landing against the seats and walls of the side of the arena that has become down. But with the lack of gravity, they're not falling fast enough to have a forceful impact. No one is getting hurt. I'm looking up, and I can see the huge four-sided replay and scoreboard that hangs from cables hooked to the roof. It's moved way over so that it's hanging against the roof. The crowd is loud, and everyone seems to be having fun, if not ecstatic about this unbelievable event happening here at the Charlotte Center tonight."

The turning of the arena continued steadily, and the roof of the building gradually became the downward direction for the fraction of gravity remaining. Fans started flying through the air toward the roof, coming to a soft landing on it. Many more seemed attracted to flying "down" to the roof and copied the action. The population of the crowd was dispersed to all the surfaces of the inside of the arena: the seating areas, the walls, the court and the floor, and the roof. Every single person in the arena was waving their arms and cheering loudly. What was happening was better than watching a ball game. A steady roar resounded throughout the volume of the arena. Vick Richards and Pat Marnham had both grabbed their microphones and reached over to a railing behind the long table they sat at. The table had gone flying into the air and wound up on the roof, leaving cables for the time clock and the horn button dangling in the air. The two announcers were determined to remain at their post and keep up the commentary.

Pat Marnham said, "More and more fans are leaping to the roof. If you don't have something to hang on to, you're going up there too."

Vick Richards said, "I'm staying right here, Pat. I'm not going anywhere."

Pat Marnham said, "I think we've gone beyond 180 degrees. The slant is now leaning over to the east side of the arena. Fans are starting to fall away from the roof. Good grief, it looks like most of the fans in the arena are now bunched up and sort of rolling across from the roof to the walls high over the seats on the east side. Now folks are jumping and dispersing across the east side of the arena, over seats and rails. Some fans are falling through the tunnels. They'll be all right."

The arena completed 270 degrees so that it was now at a right angle, making the seating on the east side "downward." Fans crowded and bunched together moved outward over the seats, walking on the backs. Fans grabbed railings and whatever was stationary while moving by each other for a space. The arena continued rotating, going into the final ninety degrees. Fans, still yelling and cheering as they moved around, began to make for either a seat or started walking their way out onto the floor. The mass spread out evenly, about half of them walking out onto the tilting basketball court. The arena completed the 360-degree rotation and came to a stop. The crowd felt the stop and roared in approval. Thirty-five thousand screaming fans stood with their arms raised up—half of them in the seats on one side of the arena, and the other half spread out over the floor. Outside, the men in the parking area, including the police and the firemen, watched as the arena began descending back into place on the part of the concrete foundation that had stayed put in the ground. Throngs of fans started hurrying through the corridors, making their way to the exits of the arena. People stopped in their tracks at the exits and watched as the arena softly landed in place on the ground. Then they began exiting quickly in loud masses, spreading out into the parking areas in all directions circling the building. Inside, most of the fans were making their way toward the exits.

The referee approached the coaches one after the other and told them he was canceling the game. Then the referee walked over to Pat Marnham and Vick Richards and told them the game was canceled.

Pat Marnham said, "We've just been told that tonight's game has been canceled, and it is for obvious reasons. I'm being told by the timekeeper that the rotation took fifteen minutes and twenty-two seconds. For you watching at home, what you've seen here tonight was not special effects. It really happened. A fantastic flipping of the entire arena. I can easily say, in all my years of covering basketball, I have never seen anything like this."

Vick Richards said, "Pat, it was the most extraordinary game I've ever commented on. I will remember this above all the games I've ever seen."

The arena announcer came on over the loudspeaker system, "Regretfully, tonight's game has been canceled. Repeat, tonight's basketball game has regretfully been canceled. Have a good night."

Pat Marnham said, "Let's see if we can get an interview with one of the players and see what he has to say. I'll stop one of them. Here's Kendrick Perkins, center for the Celtics. Kendrick, what do you think of tonight's game?"

Kendrick Perkins said, "Oh, it was unbelievable. Truly incredible. What happened here was a phenomenon. I've played basketball a long time, and I've never seen anything like this."

Pat Marnham said, "Do you agree with the official's decision to cancel the game?"

Kendrick Perkins said, "Uh, yeah. I guess he did what he felt he had to. I mean, he had to call the game off because so many people were leaving the building."

Pat Marnham said, "All right, Kendrick. Thank you. Good game, or should I say, good quarter, at least. Kendrick Perkins, everyone. And looking around the arena, people have cleared out of here pretty fast.

Like he said, the official couldn't help calling the game off, so many people were leaving the arena."

Vick Richards said, "I think it was the right decision by the official, Pat."

Pat Marnham said, "So that's it for tonight, folks. Tonight's matchup canceled because of incredible circumstances. And I wonder how this is going to look in the standings. This has been Pat Marnham and Vick Richards for CNBC. Have a good night and a pleasant tomorrow."

Raw and Uncensored,
the Beelzebub Interview

He is everywhere. He is horror. He is ancient. He is the unknown. He is the undead. He is the unexpected. As you go about your happy life, you don't know if one day he may appear to you and take your life, making you a believer of his evil purposes in your dying moments. He is the demon. He is called by the name Beelzebub.

Richard Hawley walked quickly along through the city's midday sidewalk traffic. Looking at his watch, he saw he was on time to make his appointment. Eager anticipation surged in him. He had been contacted and propositioned to write a novel, specifically a biography. He was told the book would be a sure thing to sell hugely. When he asked who the book was being written about, the person over the phone had simply said, "You'll find that out at the interview."

They had added, "The reason I've chosen you for my writer, Mr. Hawley, is I have faith in you. I've done some research on you, and you are perfect for the job. You will be paid handsomely for completing the book, along with a very large percentage of the royalties."

It had been almost a year since he had last worked. Lately, he was thinking his life as a freelance writer was over. He felt alive again to be doing something. By the sound of it, he would make a bundle. It sounded like some kind of old millionaire businessman who wanted to write his memoirs. There was a possibility he had been propositioned by someone famous.

Richard Hawley found the address, a tall office building. He entered and made way to the elevators. He glanced at the directions he had made himself on a slip of paper.

"Thirty-third floor, end of hallway," it said.

He rode the elevator up and stepped out into the thirty-third floor. Walking down the hallway, he noticed there were no businesses open behind the glass doors and all the other doors had no signs on them, as if all the occupants had recently moved out. However, at the end of the hall, he came upon what he was looking for.

A sign on the door said, "The Brooking Agency."

Hawley turned the doorknob and stepped in. There was a man in a suit sitting behind a desk. Hawley stood there for a slightly awkward pause, expecting the man to respond to him some way.

He spoke out, "I'm Richard Hawley."

The man behind the desk made no response whatsoever and kept staring blankly forward. Hawley then noticed what he was looking at was a mannequin. Suddenly, the floor of the entire office—except for a rectangular section on which Hawley was standing—dropped down and backward, swinging at a ninety-degree angle. It was all one huge elaborate trapdoor with the desk and the mannequin sitting at it secured to the "floor." Hawley tried to keep from panicking as his head swam with vertigo and his arms, one holding onto a briefcase, flailed to his sides. He instinctively turned back around to grab the doorknob and exit quickly but found there was no doorknob on this side and the door was shut and secure. He judged that there was more than a fifty-foot drop beneath him. He hadn't time to start looking at what was at the bottom of this trick section of the building he was in before the rectangular section of the floor holding him up began retracting into the wall underneath the door with a smooth "whirring" machine sound.

Now he panicked. He dropped his briefcase, and it glided downward. He made fleeting glances in every direction, desperately seeking something to grab or jump to. Nothing. This was it. He knew he was going to fall. He stood with his heels on the last remaining six-inch-wide margin of floor as it steadily retracted, frantically pressing his back against the knobless door. The floor came out from under his feet, and he fell, screaming as he went down, "Aughghghghghghgh!"

He fell for more than what must have been one hundred feet and exploded onto a soft surface.

Gripped with the realization that he had not fallen to his death, he gasped in relief. He had hit an airbag. A huge hand behind a huge desk pushed a button, and the airbag quickly began to deflate. As the airbag deflated around him, he felt floor beneath. He looked around, orienting himself. He was in a large, well-furnished room with fine wooden furniture, paintings on the wall, and luxurious handwoven rugs. At one side of the room was a huge, ornate desk that was made out of gold and carved wood. Behind it was a humanoid thing with the head of a bird and arms and chest covered with black-and-white feathers. Hawley's first thought was this thing was some kind of artificial mannequin, like the one he had just seen upstairs.

But then it moved slightly and spoke through the beak in a deep, loud, and clear voice, "Good afternoon, Mr. Hawley."

Hawley stepped off of the deflated airbag onto the floor and very slowly and cautiously made a few steps toward the man-thing with a deep consternation on his brow. Getting closer, he saw it better. He panicked and backed off.

He screamed, "Aughghghgh!"

He looked around him in a frenzy to find a way out of the room.

It spoke again, "Mr. Hawley, there is no need for you to be frightened of me. Please come and have a seat."

It motioned with its hand to a chair in front of the desk. Hawley did not immediately overcome his horror.

He yelled, "What are you? Where am I? Let me go!"

It said, "I'm who hired you to write the biography. Again, you have no need to fear me. This is a business proposition. Please, come and have a seat. We have work to do. You might want to pick up your briefcase. It fell before you did."

Hawley stared intently at the man-thing. It was huge, about six feet and eight inches, and frightening. It had huge black eyes, a black-and-white face, with a long beak and large, black hands. The skin underneath the feathers was white in some places, black in others. Hawley's mentality was starting to change and becoming less horrified. He had never seen anything unexplainable in his life. And now here he was, facing a magical beast of some sort.

He spoke to it, "You want me to write a book for you? What are you?"

It said, "I am Beelzebub. Beelzebul. Beelzeboul. Beelzebuth. Belzebuth. Baalzebub. Ba'al-zebub. The Prince of Beasts. And Lord of the Flies. There is more than one way to say my name. I am a demon, not a man. I've brought you here, Mr. Hawley, to divulge facts about my existence so that you may write a biography, just as we agreed over the phone."

Hawley stepped closer. The situation was coming into focus. He had, indeed, been hired by a demon to write his memoirs. He was not dreaming. He was overcoming his fear of the demon, although the shrill, horrid bird face was difficult to get used to. He slowly made to the chair and sat down. He couldn't help staring intently at the demon.

He said, "This is remarkable."

The demon said, "Now, are you all right, Mr. Hawley? That's good. Again, you left your briefcase over there. Is there anything you would like? A drink, perhaps? There is the bar."

The demon pointed to a small bar in the wall stocked with bottles of expensive very old liquors.

Hawley walked back to collect his briefcase off the collapsed airbag. It then retracted automatically into a compartment in the wall at the base of the floor.

Hawley said, "I don't mind if I do," and fixed himself a whiskey on ice. He drank it and started to feel better, although still rather bewildered by the situation. He sat back down and opened his briefcase, taking out a pen and a notebook. The demon sat for a pause with a reflective look on his face.

He began dictating, "First of all, let me say, Mr. Hawley, thank you for coming. I apologize for the unusual circumstances at the door. I did not want you to see me face-to-face without making sure you would not run in fear. I have decided to have a book written about myself for this purpose. To put it simply—publicity. People are not acknowledging me enough in this day and age. They are forgetting that I exist now just like I always have. Many have never heard my name. I am not a music or film star that has faded away to be forgotten. I am the powerful and immortal Beelzebub. In biblical times, if even the name Beelzebub was said, it would cause a commotion, and people would burn incense and repeat chants to purify the surroundings. It was thought that by saying my name, I could be summoned and cause death and suffering. In this digital, wireless, satellite age of now—the 'new millennium,' as they say—the average person seems to think the name Beelzebub means some kind of witch or something ancient that is dead and is of no importance. I'm tired of not being taken seriously. I would like to at least see a number of people informed as to who and what I am. So I am starting with a book. After this, though it may sound comical, Mr. Hawley, I may consider manipulating several people in Hollywood to make a movie about me. I need for people to know that I have changed as history and civilization have progressed. Gone are the days of me parading in the flames of a village bonfire in the form of a goat-headed man-beast to 'rouse up the peasants' and spread disease. I am the new Beelzebub. Modernization and technology does not protect men from my ability to create horror, terrorize, kill, and manipulate them. I have ruined kingdoms and brought about war to the earth. I am more powerful than any mere mortal can become. I am essential in that I bring about great changes. Without evil, there is no good, and without good, there is not evil.

"Well, where do I start? Long, long ago I was not a demon. I was an angel. I was worshiped by many as the Philistine, god of Ekron. That era is gone and forgotten. Those were ancient times. Very ancient. Many people confuse me with Lucifer. I am not Lucifer. I am a lesser demon. I was recruited by Lucifer when he was cast from heaven to command demons in hell. Since then I am evil. I am the next most powerful to Lucifer. I do his bidding. From Lucifer, I learned how to tempt men's pride by promising them wealth and power, only to steal back everything from them in the end and have them killed ironically for believing that I would give them something. I use lies and deceit to control men's wills. I can make almost any man no matter how wise or powerful believe in my lies, twisting him to serve my purpose.

"I will tell you now about the fall of Camelot. I destroyed the Kingdom of Camelot by imprisoning Merlin, tempting Lancelot to betray Arthur by falling in love with Guinevere, and causing his son,

Modred, to rise against Arthur and kill him. The Kingdom of Camelot was thriving. All of England knew of Arthur and his Round Table. Merlin was in his magical room on a night of the full moon, using the moonlight as energy in performing a very powerful incantation. He burned crow's feet and hung strings of hollowed sheep eyes. As the wind began blowing in a whirlwind around his castle spire, he read chants from an ancient book of magic. I never knew what the desired effect of Merlin's spell on that night was, but he read the wrong verses and mistakenly opened a portal that traversed the entire distance over Europe and the Middle East to where I was, in Canaan. I was sitting in my tent with the floor covered by rugs and pillows, being entertained by seven belly dancing women removing veils. With a burst of wind and a plume of smoke rising up from the floor in the middle of the circle of belly dancers, the portal appeared. Through the portal, I gazed at him, and he stared back at me. Immediately, I could tell he was trying to close the portal and that the magical spell he had conjured was out of control. To me he was nothing more than a clumsy old man dressed in a ridiculous robe and hood, holding candles and babbling verses he didn't know the meaning of. I flew through the portal, leaving Canaan thousands of miles behind and appeared as a beast-man with the head of a bull, nostrils flaring, eyes wide open and glowing, horns on my head, arms raised outward, materialized from the chest up, and levitating high above the floor of the room in his castle spire. I screamed horrifyingly loud and swung my arms at him. He dodged about the spire, throwing explosions at me, grabbing garlic and ivy wreath shoots, waving them at me and lighting them on fire, all the while reciting wind power chants to thwart me. He finally realized I was a powerful demon whom he could not control and dropped to his knees, bowing his head far down and holding his arms up in surrender.

"He said, 'Have mercy on me, oh, devil! I did not wish to disturb you. Surely, you can forgive a wizard?' I said to him, 'Stand up. Who are you and what castle is this?'

"He familiarized me with where I had flown to. So this was the powerful King Arthur's kingdom. I had heard of him, and so was the wizard. The wizard asked me who I was, but I told him he need not know. I told him to be less careless when casting his spells and pretended to vanish away, but instead, I became a mouse and stayed in the room.

Merlin's mistaken summoning had aroused my curiosity. I had come unto the Kingdom of Arthur, whose fame was spreading all over England. There was work to be done here. My presence was meant to be.

"Existing as the mouse, I scurried from the spire to the dining hall, to the Round Table, to the battlements, and all throughout the knights' chambers as well as Arthur and Guenevere's chamber. I learned much about the strength and victory of Camelot. The king was not only a great warrior with a magical sword, a powerful wizard, a beautiful wife, and the finest nobility of loyal knights in all England—he was quite the mediator whose diplomatic tongue won over rival kings. If Arthur continued to have success in recruiting knights to the Round Table and securing diplomatic relationships with other kingdoms, there existed the possibility that all of England could form a strong unity. In the dining hall and at the Round Table, the quest for the Holy Grail was brought up frequently. A unified England under the rule of Arthur or a joint rule of a number of kings would create an army capable of world conquest. With their fascination for the Grail and the Holy Land mixed with their ignorance of that land and its people, I knew that a unified England waging war to take over the Holy Land would be more powerful and more successful. With deceit and manipulation of many kings, I had caused the Crusades. Through misinterpretation of the Bible and ridiculous beliefs, such as the belief in the Holy Grail, thousands of young soldiers were sent to their death in the quest to take back the Holy Land. If Camelot were ended, it would weaken England. I realized my presence in the court was very strategic. I would not allow Arthur to thrive and unite England. I would bring about corruption and the demise of Camelot.

"In Merlin's spire, I watched as he concocted and used many elixirs, learning of each one's magical effect. Sir Lancelot obviously had an affinity for the queen, but his dignity and loyalty to Arthur kept him from ever making advance on her. He would never betray his king unless he were corrupted. I transformed into a black cape one night and removed a bottle of Merlin's elixir that would cast a love spell. I carried it to Lancelot's chamber and poured it on the bedsheets while he slept. It evaporated, and he breathed the magical fumes all night. The next day, when he saw Guenevere, he finally broke his code and took her aside passionately. She was surprised. She agreed to meet him in the forest and made up a story that she was going for a horse ride alone. That day was the beginning of their affair.

"I knew that Merlin was to be attributed much of the creation of the kingdom. He had educated Arthur from the time he was a boy. With him gone, I could corrupt Camelot. I had to do something with Merlin before he learned of Lancelot and Guenevere. He regularly visited the Lady of the Lake, where Excalibur had come from. He consorted with her, frequently teaching her his magic charms. Over the course of their friendship, Merlin had taught her much of his magic, making her as powerful as he. He never had any idea that she could become unfriendly toward him. Again, I took a bottle of elixir from Merlin's shelves—a potion that would cause enmity and mistrust where existed friendship. I came upon the Lady of the Lake as she slept in her underwater dwelling, entering her mind and creating a dream in which I came to her as one of the undead inhabitants of Avalon.

"I told her, 'Lady, you must not trust the magician. He is trying to use you to find a way to take over Avalon. He plans to use Avalon for his knights so that they may go to it and be healed when they are hurt in battle. He will use Avalon for his own purpose and make the undead who live there serve him.'

"As she slept, I poured the potion over her, and she breathed it in as she dreamed. I made an image of Merlin appear in the dream. He came upon the inhabitant of Avalon, raised his arms, and disabled him with a magical flash of light, then raised a sword and killed him. Merlin then reached out his hand and took the Lady of the Lake by the arm, leading her from the lake and out over land, far away. He took her to a cave fortified at the mouth with iron bars and locked her in, out of her element, on dry land, imprisoning her. He told her that he would have servants bring her food and tend to her, but she could never come out.

"When the Lady of the Lake woke the next day, the spell was in full effect on her. She was struck with a sinister mistrust of Merlin. To contradict what she had dreamed, she searched the land, found a cave, and built iron gates that would resist magical forces at the mouth. The next time Merlin visited her, she took him to it, telling him she had something she wanted him to see, innocently. To Merlin's shock, she pushed him in and locked the gate shut. She told him he would be provided for with food and kept in prison indefinitely. She left Merlin staring through the iron bars in disbelief.

"Arthur's son by his own half sister, Modred, appeared at Camelot and was allowed to become a knight. I came to Modred in a dream as a seraph and told him that he was destined to inherit the kingdom for his own. I told him that Arthur had intentionally bedded his own half sister so that she would bear an offspring to him that would serve him undauntedly. Arthur eventually learned of Guenevere's infidelity and Lancelot's betrayal. Lancelot stole away to his own castle in Wales with Guenevere, and Arthur's men laid siege to the castle. Many men were killed. Lancelot went in exile in France. Arthur followed him, leaving Guenevere at Camelot. Arthur returned to Camelot, having received message that Modred claimed the kingship for his own. Then father and son faced each other in mortal combat, army-to-army, man-to-man. They engaged. In Arthur's haste, he dropped Excalibur and the magical scabbard that would keep him from dying of injury in battle. He stabbed Modred through the heart with a spear as Modred simultaneously killed the king with a great blow of a sword through the brain. Camelot fell, and Arthur's body was taken by barge to Avalon. I flew from the battlefield, strewn with the dead bodies of fallen great knights, in the form of a hawk, ascending from the landscape of the kingdom fallen in tragedy and irony that I had caused with my own deceitful lies.

"In the year 1348, I brought the bubonic plague to Europe, spreading over the entire continent what came to be known as the Black Death. In the Gobi Desert in China existed a region in which the rats bore fleas that carried the bacteria that causes bubonic plague. It was a very sparsely populated area, and for years and years the rats with the fleas had existed, causing occasional deaths. I knew that if introduced to crowded European cities, the disease would cause epidemics. I gathered groups of rats and by shipping crates and wagons moved them to port cities, where I scurried them on to merchant ships bound for European destinations. The first outbreak was among an army surrounding the Italian-occupied City of Caffa in the Black Sea. As many of the soldiers became ill and died, the commanding officer engaged a strategy to catapult the corpses over the walls into the city. From that plague began breaking out among the Italians.

Many fled in ships to dock in Genoa and other Italian ports, but by fleeing Caffa, they had brought the plague with them. The Black Death from Italy spread all over Europe. Of the ninety million souls that populated Europe, almost half—forty million—died the Black Death. It was the second largest death toll in history. Only the sixty million casualties of World War II was greater.

"In cities and towns, so many were dying that there was a breakdown of social order. Fear of contracting disease caused husbands to abandon their wives, brothers to disavow their own brothers, and parents to abandon their own children. Livestock roamed the countryside free from farms. Houses and buildings left deserted could be rummaged through by looters. The invention of the microscope and the science of microbiology would come centuries later. People's ignorance of germs led to massive superstitious beliefs and misconceptions about the plague. Some people believed that God was bringing about the end of the world and eventually everyone would die. Some believed the plague came from gases released from hell by Satan in huge cracks of the ground during earthquakes. Some believed the stench from diseased people and corpses was what caused illness and carried perfumes and incense to burn when encountering foul air. The Black Death got its name from the condition of black, dead, and decomposing flesh appearing on the victim—the stench of which surrounded them as they still lived. Some thought merely looking at a person stricken would cause plague. This belief prompted doctors to wear bizarre bird suits with red-shaded eye holes when coming near victims.

"The image of the bird head with beak protruding forward came from stories that spread because of people witnessing appearances of me at night hovering over graveyards or perching on church steeples in the form of a giant bird man-beast. Mistakenly, I became associated with flocks of pigeons, which in turn became a symbol of good that thwarted plague. Some people decided to adopt an Epicurean manner during the plague, and 'eat, drink, and be merry for tomorrow we die,' concluding that since everyone would die, they may as well indulge themselves in their last days. They engaged in feasts of gluttony and sexual endeavors in massive parties.

"In Spain, Italy, Britain, Scandinavia, and Bavaria, all over Europe, were morbid scenes of dead bodies lying in the streets. Dogs were seen eating corpses. Huge pits were dug at cemeteries, and bodies carried on carts were thrown in. Bodies were amassed in large piles and lit on fire. Whenever I would encounter a burning pile of corpses, I would fly into the flames and appear in the form of a laughing bird man-beast.

Gyrating, spinning, and waving my arms chaotically holding a skull in either hand, I would horrify the onlookers, sending them fleeing in terror. This was my Death Dance. By the year of 1350, the plague had taken its course, and it dwindled into remission, only to break out in rare incidents thereafter. I had succeeded in turning Europe into a nightmare of massive death.

"Centuries later, sciences advanced, including the advent of the microscope, and there came a knowledge of microorganisms. Even doctors had been completely innocent to what was killing people during the plague. As technology changed, civilization and brought a new era for mankind. I too would undergo change. Their advances in medicine and machines would give humans new power over their own destiny. Many would adopt the disposition that they no longer had to fear things such as demons, scoffing at beliefs they considered to be superstitious and outdated, meanwhile having more devotion, hope, trust and love for their new sciences and systems. But mankind will never be safe from me. I will always have the power to kill, terrorize, and ravage man's faith. I decided with the coming of the new age of machine that I would use men's inventions against them—that I would kill them in terror using the very machines they made.

"History has long asked the question who was to blame for sinking the *Titanic*. I sunk the *Titanic*. I was on the ship as it steamed into the Atlantic from Queenstown, Ireland, in April 1912, taking the unassuming identity of a custodian. Word of man's largest moving object ever created had spread worldwide as it had towered in the building frames at Belfast Harbor. The building design was original, separating the hull into sixteen independent, watertight compartments. Because of this, they named it the 'unsinkable,' even before it took its maiden voyage. Many wealthy, well-known people were onboard its first trip to New York. The stage was set for the perfect disaster. I would stab mankind in its confidence and once again make humans feel my terrible, murderous wrath. I would make the floating fortress, the so-called 'unsinkable' into a gigantic, tilting iron coffin and the North Atlantic an icy graveyard.

"On April 14, as *Titanic* steamed upon the open ocean, I created an electromagnetic disturbance, which came over the equipment in the radio room as the voice of an executive with the White Star line who identified himself and instructed for the representative onboard to instruct Captain Smith to engage full power and maintain top speed. At twenty-one knots, the ship would have insufficient turning distance to avoid a collision with an iceberg with limited sighting distance at night. The captain knew the chance he was taking as he watched the sun set over the western horizon that evening. In the darkness of the night, I stood on the top deck and transformed into a bird. I flew ahead and cross-searched a great, wide expanse of ocean until I came upon a massive, solitary iceberg. The chance of one this size being directly in the path of the ship was astronomical. I looked upon it, determining its fate as a mass of icy death. I took my form of a giant man-beast and levitated above the water facing the iceberg, conjuring a great demonic force in the water surrounding it. Whirlpools swirled deep in the water and created a current that began pushing it steadily in the direction of the path of the *Titanic*. I guided it through the water for hours with my demonic force. As the ship came closer, I flew back to it then flew in a path directly forward, determining an exact collision point where I positioned the iceberg. When the iceberg came in to view, it was impossible for the ship to turn to miss it. It glided into its fatal contact like a slow, lumbering whale swimming into a great harpoon.

"There was little reaction at first. The impact had been felt by only some passengers, but inevitably with too many compartments breached and leaking, the bow began to sink and panic began emerging. Captain Smith stood mortified by the impact of the decision he had made alone in the deserted wheelhouse. He could only go down with his ship. I took the form of the man who was the company representative and burst into the wheelhouse, screaming at the captain, 'I told you, don't make this ship go full speed! I told you!'

"He screamed back, 'What? Coward! I'll kill you!'

"The captain lurched for my throat, strangling the neck and throwing me against the wall. With a sense of ironic finality, I caught a sinister sneer on my lips and began laughing as I transformed into my true image of a wild-eyed, horned, and feathered horrid demon, 'Ha-ha-ha-ha-ha-ha-ha-ha. Ha-ha-ha-ha-ha-ha-ha-ha-ha…'

"The captain stumbled back on his heels, horrified and unbelieving, as the water burst into the room. I laughed one long, continuous evil laugh as he drowned, unable to stop staring in disbelief at my demonic form. The climax of the horror was when more than a thousand panicking passengers of the 1,523 who couldn't get on the lifeboats swarmed to the back end of the ship and clutched one another in futility, facing inevitable death as the great monstrosity tilted steeper and steeper upward, being raised by the weight of the sinking front. I circled above them as a bird and burst out before them, appearing as a towering, flaming demonic man-beast with my horns and glowing eyes. I laughed my deafening, shrill, demonic laugh as I danced, spinning and waving my two flaming skulls. The visage of me and the truth that I killed them all was their last realization as they fell, crashing into each other, metal surfaces or landing in the water or ending up in the freezing water clinging to the last of the ship as it dropped flat after breaking in half, then tilted one last time upward, and sank. In only minutes, the frenzied mass of splashing, screaming victims turned into a morbid, silent diameter of floating, pale corpses. I had turned man's great creation into a tortuous death contraption.

"I destroyed the largest ship ever built in its time. Years later, the *Hindenburg* was constructed in a mammoth hangar in Germany. At 804 feet in length, it was the largest airship ever made. I decided I would destroy it also. The owner of the *Hindenburg's* company, Hugo Echener, was a celebrated entrepreneur/mogul who had become a hero flying around the world in the Graf Zepplin. Zepplins were faster than boats. The Atlantic could be traversed by a zeppelin in a fraction of the time of a ship at sea.

They were traveled in by the elite rich and were thought to be safer than traveling in airplanes. But the *Hindenburg* was never safe. In fact, it was a floating disaster waiting to happen with its hydrogen gas cells and highly flammable outer skin. The design was simple: end-to-end bowl-shaped hydrogen gas cells separated by huge aluminum alloy *O* ring frames. Cotton cloth covered the framing. What made it unsafe was the metallic doping compound used to paint the entire exterior. For purposes of resisting wind, rain, and heat from sunshine, three highly flammable chemicals comprised the doping agent: iron oxide, cellulose nitrate, and powder aluminum. Iron oxide is flammable, cellulose nitrate is gunpowder, and powder aluminum is used as a burning fuel for rockets. Painted with these, the best possible chemicals for the aspect of functioning, the *Hindenburg* had a beautiful, sleek silver appearance—although it was virtually like a hovering firecracker, a disaster waiting to happen.

"On May 6, 1937, the *Hindenburg* floated in majestically to its hangar port at Lakehurst, New Jersey. As usual, a crowd of admirers with reporters and photographers had gathered to see the landing of the technical marvel. I had come from Europe, acting as an anonymous well-to-do businessman, mingling with the other passengers and smoking cigars in the smoking room. I slipped through the catwalks among the frame rafters as the zeppelin hovered, releasing its towing ropes. I transformed into a huge flame and flew into the framework up to the top of the back end of the airship, igniting the flammable skin. When the fire spread and ignited the first hydrogen gas cell, the whole airship combusted into a mammoth torching inferno. I danced, contorting, convulsing, and jumping from frame to frame inside through the white hot blaze. It was perfect timing to have the great zeppelin burst into flames to the sheer horror and amazement of the onlookers just before it landed. Witnesses would later describe the tragedy to be like 'looking at hell itself burning.' With a thunderous sound, it came to the ground as passengers and crew dropped to the ground under it, escaping the fire. It collapsed, and the metal framework caved in—a twisted, broken, and burning heap. Miraculously, two-thirds of the ninety-seven aboard survived. News of the disaster spread worldwide as fast as the fire itself had combusted. The disaster made such a great impact in the media that people stopped traveling in zeppelins altogether. Hugo Echener lost most of his fortune as all of his zeppelins were grounded, and he faded from public view. The *Hindenburg* marked the end of passenger zeppelin travel. And I developed an affinity for destroying man's greatest creations.

"Hell is actually much larger than the earth itself. It existed in a limited, smaller sense before the earth began. Hell develops and grows with the passing of the history of the world. Events that happen in the world mirror events in hell. Whatever that is evil—calamities, disasters, horrors, wars, and tortures—happened in scenes in hell before taking place in the world. Only in hell they were ten times worse, on a ten times larger scale, and with ten times the pain and suffering. Hell is a polluted, burning, violent, and decrepit wasteland where living souls could not exist without dying. Whatever is good or pleasurable, such as good food, does not exist anywhere in hell. Ghettos on earth have vast relative wastelands in hell. Imagine the Casbah being the size of an entire country where tortured souls exist in dire poverty in that twisted, three-dimensional maze of infamy among rats and vermin for eternity, never to see the light of the sun. For every great building and city ever built is a paradoxical civilization of wreckage and ruin sprawling over vast distances in hell.

"Early cultures believed ignorantly that hell existed downward, underground. That mankind has matured a level is illustrated by the repudiation of this belief, just as it matured a level when it gave up thinking the world was flat. The truth is that hell exists, although in other dimensions, upward from earth. In a magnetic field yet undiscovered by science stretching within part of the distance of the solar wind are seven spheres, which decrease in size from the first to the last. These invisible seven spheres are the seven descending levels of hell. They counter-rotate in relation to each other, starting with the rotation of the earth. The center points of all eight, including the earth, remain at a constant distance from one another trailing into the solar wind as it follows behind the earth's orbit in a curved 'tail' stretching approximately thirty earth lengths. Each sphere's surface protrudes into the consecutive, the surface of the first protruding a depth of 240 miles into the earth's surface. All the spheres intersect in two-sided contact lens shapes of lessening depths. Each descending sphere has an axis countertilting exactly to the consecutive so that they stand in line at nearly a slender X formation viewed sideways during the summer and winter solstice, giving a little differentiation in the tilts for the tailing distance in the orbit and in the center points contained in the slight curve. At the spring and fall equinox, the eight axes form disconnected *W* shapes viewed from front or back. The eight equators fluctuate against the consecutive in tilting, circular gyro motion as the train progresses in the orbit. The diameter of earth is 7,907 miles. The diameter of the first hellsphere is 480 less at 7,427 miles. The diameter of each hellsphere is the diameter of the one before minus twice the depth it protrudes into the one before. The diameter of the seventh is only 1,440 miles. From the perspective of earth, the hellspheres trail outward in the orbit; however, within the alter dimensions of hell, the seven constitute a vast maze of chambers and landscapes with portals, staircases, cliffs, and pits all leading downward. Dante was correct in guessing that the lower the location in hell, the worse it is. Gravity itself is much greater in the bottom levels than on earth, lending to nightmarish conditions where bent-over souls are eternally tortured. The concept that hell lies in a downward direction originates with what was overheard from demons describing it.

"So you see, there are physical, scientific properties having to do with hell. Mathematically, very complex equations are involved with the relating proportions of the hellspheres to the earth and to the distance of the solar wind. The proportions relate further to the speed of their rotations, which create a special energy of great magnitude that is the architecture of a time warp field. Further fantastically complicated mathematical equations represent relations with the alter dimensions at the other side of the time warp to physical factors of the time warp. The warp contains all the elements of space, energy, matter, and time in a 'spinning' frame, whereby they shift into and become the other, creating the alter dimensions of the afterworld of hell. Lucifer, I, and other powerful demons know how to traverse from one world to the other using not magical but scientific means. This is difficult for humans to comprehend and difficult to explain. There really is no magic. What powers we use you could call 'super science.' We need no machines or devices. Lucifer is vastly intelligent. His great mind dwarfs any man that has ever lived, even a genius such as Einstein. The Bible states that Lucifer was God's greatest creation and that his wisdom was made to be far beyond all men. The day will come very far in the future from now when men will gain the knowledge and technology that will empower them to reach hell without dying. When that day comes, there will be a war far more devastating than any war ever. Hell will open up, and all the evil built up throughout history will reign terror upon the living. It will be a war between hell and earth in which Lucifer will demand the entire world shall come to an end, for mankind can never be allowed to challenge his power.

"In one of the bottom levels of hell is a vast chamber, which has several roads that are wide as a great river lined with towering stone columns connected with arches at the height of skyscrapers. Where the roads come together is a great circular floor of raging flames. In the middle of the flaming floor is a stone platform with a stone throne. At a distance in front of the throne is another stone seat facing the throne. It is there that Lucifer meets me to discuss serious matters. As the world went into the turn of the twentieth century, I met Lucifer there. I listened attentively to what he told me, the flames of the flaming floor whipping back and forth, like ripples on a lake with the wind, from the sound of his booming voice, 'Great technological changes are coming for mankind. With these changes, all the people of civilization will look to their governments and wonder how to define authority. People will be susceptible to new ideas. We will use their time of adjusting to bring about great destruction. As they experience their new methods of transportation and communicate more efficiently globally, it will only take one person to lead millions and bring about war. A catalyst we will use to cause evil to occur during the good of their new civilization. We will bring about the greatest war of all and kill humans with their new weapons of destruction. Go out into the world, Beelzebub, and search all nations and cities. Search the aristocracy, the bourgeois, and the proletariat to find our catalyst. We will allow him to rise within a government and secure power over a nation to bring about destruction worse than ever seen on earth.'

"I searched the nations of the world. Europe was the center of the world, and if any one country stood out that would have the people with the right mentality and the resources to turn against the rest of the countries, it was Germany. It would be the strategic one in the new age of machine because Germany itself is like a machine. In December of 1909, my search led me to the fringe of obscurity—a homeless shelter called Asyl fur Obdachlose in Meidling, Vienna, Austria. There I found a twenty-year-old young man whose ideals of patriotism for Germany and anti-Semitism were well spoken among the men in casual conversation groups at night in the shelter. This was the young Adolph Hitler, down on his luck and hit with poverty. He was forming what he would later call his 'worldview' by adopting opinions he read from tabloids such as *Ostara*, which carried racial, anti-Semitic messages that were becoming popular especially among the working class of Austria and Germany. I, posing as another homeless man, spent time talking with Hitler to find that he could argue a point convincingly and had a way of speaking that would grip the attention of those listening. I decided from there to learn about his past and watch him as his life progressed.

He enlisted in the German Army when World War I broke out while living in Munich. He was a bicycle messenger in combat in the trenches. It was a dangerous position that earned him several commendations. In October 1918, his regiment fighting at Comines, France, was hit by a British assault using mustard gas. Hitler was temporarily blinded and sent to a military hospital in Pasewalk near Stettin, in Pomerania. I acted as another soldier with the same condition so I could confide with him. I told him that I, also, had come from his hometown of Linz, and he asked me when was I last there and what news was to be heard about Linz.

"I said, 'Nothing in particular. There was a thing about a crazy quack of a doctor. A Jewish man. Dr. Bloch. He was found to have poisoned to death several of his patients.' Hitler lay in bed shocked at hearing this and said only, 'Really, that is incredible.'

"I knew that Dr. Bloch had treated his mother's fatal cancer, and Hitler had developed a suspicion of him over the years. In the hospital, news spread of the revolutionary movement that forced the government of Germany to admit defeat at having a badly hurt army and surrender to the allies, ending World War I. Hitler, like many soldiers who did not want to surrender, considered the revolutionaries to be 'a gang of criminals assuming control of the Fatherland.' From this time, Hitler's pathological anti-Semitism grew, and his idea of grandeur to be the one to 'save' Germany began.

"Upon joining the small Nazi party, Hitler quickly gained status as one of the top leaders with his charismatic beer hall speaking. The party grew in number, and on November 8, 1923, he made an attempt to overthrow the government, a putsch, in which head of the provincial

Bavarian government Gustav Von Kahr and associates were taken hostage. From there, six hundred armed Sturmabteilungen (SA, Nazi paramilitary) marched to the center of Munich the following day, to be met and outnumbered by the police. Sixteen Nazis were killed, and Hitler was put in prison at Landsberg. Within a few days, I assumed the identity of a guard and entered his cell. By then I was convinced Hitler could be the one to take over Germany. He was the catalyst.

"I appeared before Hitler to his surprise, gazing across the cell at him. He said, 'Was! Wer sind Sie?

Wie sind Sie hereingekommen?' ('What! Who are you? How did you get in here?')

"To show him I was a demon, I disappeared and reappeared in different areas across the cell. He was shocked and said, 'Was sind Sie? Ein Geist? Was wollen Sie mit mir?' ('What are you? A ghost? What do you want with me?')

"I said to him, 'Sie haben keine Ursache, mir zu furchten, Herr Hitler. Ich bin dein Fruend. Ich bin geleommen, um dir anzuraten.' ('You have no reason to fear me, Herr Hitler. I am your friend. I have come to advise you.')

"He said, 'And you are a spirit come to guide me while I am in prison?' 'Yes, Hitler. You have done the right thing with your putsch. You have given the Nazi what they need for a start. You will not be in prison long, I promise, and after you are released, you will bring the Nazi into power. Mark my words, Hitler, you are the one to save Germany. You need to have your "worldview" written in a book so your views can be read by many people. Call it *Mien Kampf* (*My Struggle*).'

"Hitler was released in only a few months and went on to become wealthy and famous from his book.

With his energetic speeches, he propelled the Nazi party into power and in 1933 became the German chancellor, assuming all power by force. After gaining absolute power, Hitler forced Czechoslovakia and Austria into annexation with Germany. Then on September 1, 1939, he invaded Poland, starting World War

II. Later, Hitler would engage France, Britain, Russia, and America. He waged World War II, involving all of Europe in the greatest destruction ever, ravaging the land with bombs and warfare and creating the nightmare of concentration camps in which millions of Jews faced inevitable death in gas chambers.

"In Berlin, there was a comedy club where a look-alike of Hitler was performing. He was a dead ringer for Hitler, not to mention being hilarious onstage. The show also had a double for Eva Braun, who was just as convincing. Posing as a guard for Hitler in his Fuhrenbunker, I suggested that he have soldiers bring the look-alikes and use them as replacements so that Hitler and Eva Braun might fake their deaths. When the Russian troops stormed into Berlin, Hitler ordered the look-alikes to take cyanide, and the bodies were taken out into the bombing and damaged enough that they could not be clearly recognized. It worked.

Russian soldiers confiscated the bodies and believed they had Hitler and Eva Braun. Hitler and Eva Braun escaped into secret tunnels that had been built in the design of the Fuhrenbunker that only he knew about. They went on to live an underground existence after the war.

"With my manipulation of important people, I brought about the final and most dramatic finale to World War II—the bombings of Hiroshima and Nagasaki. In 1939, I wrote an anonymous letter to Albert Einstein, saying that I was a German scientist who did not wish to be identified. I urged him that key German scientists were on the brink of creating the first atomic bomb. That prompted Einstein to correspond with F. D. Roosevelt, urging him to organize the Manhattan Project and beat the Germans in making the first bomb. The genius Robert Oppenheimer led the project. As the war came to an end in Germany, the work of scientists Werner von Braun and Dieter Kolff had succeeded in making, up to that point, the most powerful weapon of the war— the A-4 rocket, capable of flying from its takeoff at Peenemunde Island in the Baltic Sea and exploding on target in London with one ton of Trialen, many times more explosive than TNT. The two scientists had conceptualized the super bomb in rocket form, but their effort was the last for the German side with Russian and American troops capturing all of Germany and taking soldiers and scientists prisoner—the official surrender coming on May 7, 1945. In Los Alamos, with six thousand people living in the desert town, success was reached with the first atomic testing, the Trinity test on July 16, 1945. Roosevelt was informed that two bombs would be created—Little Boy, which fired one piece of uranium

235 into another, and Fat Man, which used plutonium 239 surrounded by high explosives.

"On August 6, 1945, Little Boy was dropped on Hiroshima. I became the bomb itself as it exploded in its firestorm, hovering high over the city. From a distance, great enough to escape the blast, I could be seen in the form of a mammoth dragon spanning outward great wings and glowing huge bulging eyes, rotating slowly in a circle and viewing the fire and destruction. The blast killed instantly seventy thousand people and suctioned buildings reduced to debris in its mushroom cloud. I saw as I looked out over the calamity, people with burning flesh were falling from their standing bodies, and others were leaping into the rivers to escape the burning only to drown in boiling water. Three days later came Nagasaki, on August 9, 1945. Again I became the bomb as it exploded, embodying the torrential horror as it loomed over the city forming a mushroom cloud at Ground Zero, killing forty thousand instantly. Again I took the form of the gigantic dragon with wings outstretched and glowing, bulging eyes, slowly rotating around and viewing the massive death. Humanity felt my wrath then as never before, and World War II ended with its unthinkable finale of destruction.

"In the late 1950s, the nuclear arms race between the Soviet Union and the United States began coming to a climax, and in 1962 came the Cuban Missile Crisis. I determined to use the circumstances to bring about a nuclear war. The Kennedy administration took office in 1961. Jupiter missiles had been placed in Turkey and Italy, and Thor missiles had been given to Great Britain in answer to Soviet medium-range and intermediate-range ballistic missiles being set up by the Soviets against those countries within the borders of Soviet bloc countries. The United States was winning the arms race with intercontinental ballistic missiles and intelligence as well as espionage efforts revealed the Soviets had not yet developed ICBMs. The missile gap was in favor of the US. Russia's leader, Nikita Krushchev, during a visit to Bulgaria, was pacing up and down his hotel room, confronting this dilemma. I had found him there, and my presence loomed in the room. I was reading his thoughts, his plans. With a telepathic message, I persuaded him, 'What if the Soviet Union used Fidel Castro's communist allegiance in Cuba and secretly set up missiles there?' Krushchev started thinking on this matter, and soon the Kremlin was making plans to do so.

"I came to Castro at one of his offices in Havana. He was sitting at a large desk, smoking a cigar.

Suddenly, I changed the desk into a large, circular two-sided desk and the room in front of Castro into what would be in back of a desk with elaborate tapestries bearing my emblems of death skulls and several dragons hanging on the wall. Then I appeared to him in demonic form. He was shocked and stood up in an attempt to flee from the room, but when he stumbled around the desk, it became the other side in a Mobius Strip effect where there was only one side contained in the two. He could not escape the position of staring at me in front of my emblems.

"I said, 'Siente te aqui, Castro, que podemos hablar.' ('Sit here and discuss matters with me, Castro.') He said, 'Quien eres?' ('Who are you?') I said, 'Soy su amigo, un conspirador.' ('I am your friend, a conspirator.') He said, 'Are you the devil?' 'A demon. Let me guide your attention to matters with the US. There is a way in which you can defy the US ultimately. If you were to allow the Soviets to station troops and build missile sites in Cuba, then the US would not think of invading your country so easily, would they?' 'Soviet missiles here?' 'Yes, Castro. You would have the power to wage war with the US,' I said to him leaning close, face-to-face over the two-sided desk. 'The Russians have already decided to consult you on this matter, Castro. Make the agreement with them. This is your chance at world domination, Castro.' I then disappeared along with the desk, the wall, and the tapestry.

"On Sunday, October 14, 1962, U-2 spy planes flying over San Cristobal in western Cuba photographed erector launchers, missile-carrying trailers, fueling trucks, and radar vans of a battalion of Soviet medium-range ballistic missiles. Further U-2 photography revealed launch sites at Remedios, Sagua la Grande, Guanajay, and others. The US suspicions had been confirmed, and the worst fear became real. The boldest move possible had been made by the Soviets. It was the first ever breech of the Monroe Doctrine, which declared for more than two centuries the entire hemisphere of North, Central, and South America off-limits to European powers. Kennedy called for a special committee ExCom (Executive Committee of the National Security Counsel) to meet in secret. Launching a military air strike against missile sites was discussed as an option. I wanted this to take place. But Kennedy and his brother, Robert, who was the attorney general, both wanted a diplomatic communication with the Soviets before reverting to military action. Kennedy prepared a speech, and on October 22, he spoke to the US and the world at large, promising a naval quarantine of Cuba and declaring the Soviets to have committed an act of war. He called on the support of NATO and appealed to the Soviets to immediately withdraw missiles from Cuba. What happened was a grave disappointment to me.

"Even though on October 27, at the blackest hour of the crises when a U-2 was shot down over Cuba by a surface-to-air missile (SAM) the Soviets in a few days recanted. Krushchev agreed in communications with Kennedy to remove all medium-range ballistic missiles and allow for ships as well as newly built missile sites to be inspected. Kennedy had dissolved the impending doom of the missile crises with his brilliant diplomacy. I had not ever confronted him. Both he and his brother were men whom I could not communicate with at all. To them, a demon was something mischievous to be thought of humorously, not a power figure. They would simply scoff at the belief that I could lead them in their affairs. I was powerless over them, they were good men. I can only convene with the wicked.

"In a last chance desperate move, I met again with Castro, making the two-sided desk appear in his office. I urged him, 'If you move forces now, Castro, you can gain control of the missile sites. There is still a chance of engaging the US. You must use the MRBMs while they are still here.' He said, 'What? My soldiers attack the Soviets? That is ludicrous. My army is greatly outmanned.' I said, 'But you can win, Castro. You must go on the offensive now. You have much to gain by launching missiles at the US.' He said, 'I cannot let you lead me anymore. The Missile Crises is over!' And with that he ran out of the office, breaking through the force of the two-sided room. I was disheveled. I had failed completely. The human race had won in maintaining peace and abstaining from using nuclear weapons. Still to this day, I am always looking to find a way to cause a nuclear war. The day may come when to everyone's surprise and horror, it happens. There is always that lingering possibility.

"With détente and the subsiding of the Cold War, I set my sights on other endeavors of destruction. It was clear that with the world superpowers stalemated in the nuclear arms race, smaller wars would happen. So it came to be with Korea and Vietnam, as the US acted on the threat of communism spreading. Also keeping me preoccupied in the 'sixties was the rioting and social unrest in the US in the face of social reform and the Afro American rights movement. With the development of the civilized world and the ever-growing need for oil, the rest of the world would become dependent on the Middle East. Tension in the Middle East in the form of hate for Israel and Muslim fundamentalist values clashing with Western culture and Christian ways was going to determine much of the violence in the world in decades to come. This I could see. It seemed the Middle East would become the center of controversy for the whole world, and from that I could exploit situations to cause calamities, disasters, wars. I needed another catalyst, another Hitler. One man to turn millions into the next Nazi party.

"Mohammed bin Laden was a wealthy construction company owner who had risen to prominence partially because of his association with the Saudi Arabian royal family, the al-Sauds. His company was worth one billion by the time one of his sons by several wives, Osama bin Laden, was born in 1957. Osama grew up being different from his brothers in that he was more of a devout Muslim than they were, spending time reading the Koran and praying. Even though he did take trips to England with his family as a boy, he never set foot on American soil and opted to go to a Muslim university: King Abdul Aziz University in Jeddah, Saudi Arabia.

"Studying at King Abdul Aziz, bin Laden began forming more sincere anti-American and hard-line Muslim fundamentalist beliefs. He began to see the Saudi government as corrupt and a puppet to US influence and domination. He read the writings of two radical Muslim fundamentalists—Abdllah Azzam and Muhammed Qutb—who were considered respected teachers of Islamic studies by some and feared as dangerous radicals by others. Bin Laden was not encouraged by his brothers to engage in such radical teachings. He was hopefully going to finish college and join his brothers in the family business, which his older brother Salem had renamed the Saudi Bin Laden Group (SBG) when the father died in a helicopter crash when Osama was just eleven years old. But bin Laden insisted on going the other way, joining radical Muslim groups and developing beliefs that violence should be used by Muslims to defend their religion.

"In December 1979, the Soviet Union invaded Afghanistan. Before the events hit the news, I came to bin Laden in his home in Jeddah in the form of a djinn. I said, 'Osama, greetings. I have come to you. You are called upon by the prophet to serve Allah. The infidels of the Soviet Union are soon to invade Afghanistan with military force. You are needed to fight in the holy jihad. You will go to Pakistan and fight the infidels in the name of Allah.' He said, 'Yes, mighty djinn. I will do what you say. Praise Allah.'

"When the war broke out, it was immediately construed as an attack on the Muslim world, even though the US declared to be allied in an effort against the Soviet Union. Thousands of sympathizers, rich and poor, from Muslim countries all over the Middle East flocked to the Afghanistan border with Pakistan willing to take arms to fight the Soviets. Bin Laden went to Peshawar, close to the Afghanistan border. He was determined to use his personal wealth to help the cause.

"In spring 1980, the town of Peshawar was seething with soldiers, spies, gunrunners, drug dealers, Afghan refugees, exiles, journalists, and thousands of sympathizers ready to join the Afghan army. The radical fundamentalist Abdullah Azzam, bin Laden's icon, came to Peshawar and met bin Laden personally. The two shared beliefs and formed a bond. They collaborated to create a behind the lines resistance force aiding the Afghan military. Bin Laden traveled back and forth from Saudi Arabia, collecting millions in donations for the cause and adding in from his own personal wealth. It was during this time that bin Laden rose to fame. He created hospitals, roads using SBG construction equipment, and training camps while many soldiers hurt in battle were given money by him as he frequented the hospitals. He even went into Afghanistan and spent time fighting at the front lines himself. He was struck by shrapnel and had to recover in his own hospital. He became a well-known hero, a legend in his own time. Every Muslim in Afghanistan and much of the Middle East came to know the name bin Laden. Sometimes he was referred to as *emir*, an Arab title of royalty.

"The Soviets withdrew from Afghanistan in 1989. They had lost the war. They were not able to overcome the loyal Muslim army of Arabs willing to die for their cause, although casualties had favored the Soviet army. The financial impact of the war on the Soviet Union eventually led to the collapse of the iron curtain and dissension of the Soviet bloc countries. Bin Laden's legend had spread throughout the Middle East, and he was greatly emboldened by the defeat. When the war ended, he formed al-Qaeda (meaning 'the base') turning the training camps he had organized into new terrorist facilities, and he took the Muslim stance to continue the holy jihad against the US, the Saudi government, and Israel.

"Bin Laden gave speeches when he returned to Saudi Arabia, and his lectures were distributed on tape.

He fell in ill favor with the Saudi government for his radical views and was exiled, finding refuge in Sudan after being invited to live there by high-ranking members of that government. During this time, bin Laden fortified al-Qaeda with weapons, men, and training camps. Other existing terrorist groups such as Hamas, Hezbollah, and Islamic Jihad began being associated with al-Qaeda and sharing tactical terrorist techniques and training. Al-Qaeda cells were started all over the world, in Europe and the US with fronts as ordinary offices. Terrorist incidents began to emerge with suspicion being given to al-Qaeda. Al-Qaeda's first attack was made in December 1992. Operatives bombed two hotels in Yemen that were housing American troops en route to Somalia for the military offensive taking place there. February 26, 1993, a truck bomb exploded in the World Trade Center, killing six and wounding over a thousand. The evidence pointed toward al-Qaeda. In October 1993, al-Qaeda furnished Somali troops with rocket-propelled grenades in fighting Blackhawk helicopters. A range of truck bomb incidents took place in 1995 and 1996 and were attributed to al-Qaeda. Bin Laden was exiled from Sudan under pressure against the government. From there he went back to Afghanistan. Al-Qaeda was strengthening, and bin Laden was becoming public enemy number one to the US. In Afghanistan, he made connections with the Muslim fundamentalist government, the Taliban. August 7, 1998, at 10:30 AM two truck bombs attributed to al-Qaeda went off minutes apart, one at the American embassy in Nairobi, Kenya, killing 201 Kenyans and 12 Americans. Four thousand people were injured. The other one exploded at Dar es Salaam, Tanzania, in front of another American embassy with not as extensive damage. The US called for the government of Afghanistan to surrender bin Laden as a criminal, but instead he was revered as a hero, and al-Qaeda grew stronger in force and more feared in reputation.

October 2000, al-Qaeda drifted a small fishing boat laden with explosives into the *USS Cole* in port at Yemen, putting a huge hole in the hull and killing seventeen.

"I came to bin Laden again in 2001. I said to him, 'Osama, it is me. I am here to advise you again.' He said, 'Mighty djinn, it is good to see you again,' and he bowed. I said, 'You have become strategically powerful, and al-Qaeda is capable of causing the greatest terrorist calamity ever. You will have your chance of waging the holy jihad against the infidels of the US. I will teach you how. Listen to me. Truck bombs can only do so much. They are limited. But if fully fueled commercial jet planes were to be hijacked and flown directly into skyscrapers, greater destruction can occur. I want you to coordinate an attack hijacking four planes and crash them into the World Trade Center, the Pentagon, and the White House all in a single attack. We will cause the greatest terrorist act ever, and you will go down in infamy.'

"He said, 'I will do as you wish, mighty djinn. We will wage jihad against the US as I have always wanted to do. Praise Allah.'

"On the morning of 9/11, I influenced the electronic metal detectors in the airports as operatives passed through, allowing several terrorists to board planes holding knives. At 8:45 AM was the height of the catastrophe as I hovered in Flight 11 as it careened into the World Trade Center. Passengers screamed frantically in their last gasp of breath and terrorist operatives said with finality, 'Praise Allah.' The plane and I exploded into the building. The north tower ignited into a huge fireball. At 9:03, I took out the south tower consecutively with Flight 175. As they burned, people stuck inside fighting for their lives saw me parade from floor to floor, dancing in demonic form holding a skull in either hand. I melted through ceiling to floor, ceiling to floor, spinning around violently and screaming a shrill, high-pitched, deafening howl in the murderous ecstasy of my Death Dance to the horrified faces of helpless victims. I knew that the firemen and police rushing into the buildings were ironically climbing to their death, but everyone was oblivious to the fact that both buildings would completely collapse. I had designed it to happen exactly that way. It was perfect: the greatest catastrophe towering high in the New York sky on that clear, fateful morning. It stunned the world.

"And now you know Mr. Hawley. I am the great Beelzebub. I am immortal. I am invincible. I will exist after this civilization is reduced to dust and rubble under the sun. No nation nor its leader is safe from me and my manipulative power. I have existed thousands and thousands of years and seen the rise and fall of every so-called great man. No mortal man has ever impressed me. While others revel in the fame and fortune of their heroes, warriors, leaders, and celebrities, I see them for what they are—nothing. Whatever level of fame, recognition, or stardom a human achieves is meaningless and does not excite me. I coldly reach out to any man, no matter how great he thinks he is, and manipulate, ruin, kill, or torture him—showing him in the end that he was merely another mortal human being. I have cavorted with most of the great villains, killers, psychopaths, and evil dictators throughout history—so many more than I have mentioned in our brief discussion—Emporer Nero, Genghis Khan, Jack the Ripper, Pol Pot, Charles Manson, Timothy McVie, to name a few. Lucifer and I together are the origin and the root of evil in this world and always have been. And evil is what compels man. Whether evil compels man more so than good is an age old subject of argument.

"No machine or creation of man's will ever be safe from my sabotage if and when I get the urge to destroy it. The space shuttle is now the greatest machine on Earth. It is ironic that it is also very easy to destroy. It is so complicated that any one of a number of problems can develop during flight and cause it to crash. It was easy to explode the *Challenger* on January 28, 1986, killing seven astronauts. I merely caused a friction to rip apart the booster rocket. I will continue to terrorize, kill, and cause catastrophes until the day comes when all life on earth comes to an end. For now, Mr. Hawley, I want recognition from the people of the world. Like I told you, I am not getting enough respect in these modern times. It is up to you to write this book. What I've told you is my story, and this is my proposition. What is your answer?"

Hawley shifted in his seat across the huge desk from the great demon. His gaze had been fixated on the demon, trancelike for the duration of the interview. There was a long pause as the two stared across the huge wooden desk at each other, questioning each other's intentions. Hawley closed his notebook and put his pen in his shirt pocket.

He suddenly felt a surge of will, boldly stood up, and blurted out to the demon, "There is no way I am ever going to write your book! You can't make me! Damn you, cursed demon!"

Beelzebub became furious. His pit viper eyes glared wildly as he stood from his seat and rounded the desk. Hawley began backing away from him.

He said forcefully, "Mr. Hawley, you don't have a choice in the matter. I chose you among many writers. Just write the book as you've been told. If you do not, there will be grave consequences for you."

The demon reached out and grabbed Hawley by the collar, holding him firmly. Hawley gasped, frozen with fear as the demon thrust his bird face close. Its eyes were huge and wild, showing bloodshot veins.

Suddenly, a roaring noise broke out in the room, like the air of a vast, open space expanding as a gigantic door opened. The room behind the demon diluted and faded out, and a scene appeared showing a long cave with men hung on the walls of both sides in solid iron shackles. There was one being stretched by the wrists and the ankles from chains hanging from the ceiling and bolted to the floor. One was in an iron mask covering his sunken head and hanging from his wrists. Another was horizontal with huge iron screws piercing into his head. The two sides of the chamber seemed to go on forever into the darkness of the background only lit with torches on the walls. Screaming men could be heard off far down in the chamber.

"This is where men who oppose me or don't do what I say end up. Don't think that medieval torture is extinct. I still use it. I invented it. Believe me, Mr. Hawley, I can make your life a living horror. You don't want to get on my bad side. Remember, you won't be able to escape me by fleeing off to some remote corner of the world. I can find you wherever you are. Just write the book. I assure you, it will make you rich. I'll be watching you. You won't see me, but I'll always be there."

The demon released his grip on Hawley's neck as the torture cave scene faded away with men's horrified howls trailing off into the distance. The interview room returned, and Beelzebub began to walk out of the building as a doorway materialized and opened onto the street outside. He took the form of a man in a business suit and began walking out. He turned and for one last time addressed Hawley.

"Think about it, Mr. Hawley, and do the right thing."

Beelzebub simply exited, differing from his usual dramatic exit in flames or deafening explosion, and Hawley was left standing there, astounded. Finally, he collected his notebook and briefcase he had dropped on the floor, straightened his hair, put on his jacket, and walked out the same doorway the demon had taken constituting the side of the building, onto the sunny street with cars honking and people walking by. He looked around, and the businessman Beelzebub had transformed into was nowhere to be seen.

Beelzebub arrived by car at Cape Canaveral Shuttle Base. He had taken the form of scientist, Dr. Kevin McGruber, an engineer in charge of design and maintenance. The real Dr. McGruber had mysteriously disappeared in a freak car accident on a bridge over the Intercoastal Waterway with no witnesses. It was the end of January 2003, and the shuttle *Columbia* was on the verge of its infamous last flight in which upon reentering the atmosphere, it disintegrated, killing seven astronauts onboard. Beelzebub, wearing a white lab coat and carrying a briefcase, walked into the hangar.

Einstein's Address to the Public of the Future

A man was sitting behind his desk in his office on a usual weekday. At exactly twelve o'clock noon, a static *click* sound emanated from thin air directly in front of his desk. The same high-pitched squeal that can be heard from a TV set came from the space. It grew louder. Suddenly, a blink of light appeared and expanded outward, just like a picture emerging on a TV screen. It grew, covering a rectangular space, a yard and a half wide by one yard in height. It shown brightly in black and white. Almost immediately an image appeared on the screen, the image of Albert Einstein, staring back sincerely with consternation on the brow. The man was astounded by the screen and stumbled around his desk to examine it. It was a hair-thin surface, which only showed from the front and nothing but transparent space could be seen from the back. He dropped back into his chair and gasped at the image of Einstein with eyes bewildered. He noticed the image was moving slightly and the face blinked. It began to speak…

"Hello. As you can guess, I am Albert Einstein. What you are seeing is an electromagnetic emittance traversing time. You can see me, but I cannot see you or any of your surroundings. This transmission is coming from the year 1951, January 21, 12:00 PM. I am at my home in Princeton, and you are on the twenty-second floor of an office building in New York City on June 21 at 12:00 PM, the year being 2001. Therefore, the time elapsed by the transmission is fifty years and six months. You'll notice that the origin of my signal is on winter solstice, and you are now at summer solstice. It was essential that the transmission could only take place on this day and be received on your day. The electromagnetic frequency being used is a very 'special' one, not on the scale of radio but higher. You could assume that this is taking an enormous amount of energy, but it isn't. My power source is a simple small generator. I am looking through a rectangular border made up of simple wire with electrodes at the four corners, which is equal in dimension to what you see. This is the mathematical formula representing this 'time warp screen' you are viewing:

$$d = \int_0^{50.5} C\left(T\left(\frac{50.5}{\theta}\right)\left(\frac{50.5}{T}\right)\right)\frac{d}{dx}$$

"The T represents time, C is the speed of light, *theta* is the position of the appearance and origin of the screen, and d represents the distance from Princeton to New York, in relation with the distance around the earth and the sun in orbit. This signal actually covers a vast distance from the circling orbits of the earth around the sun for fifty and a half years. The direction and the fact that I could predict and locate a man in a room of a building in New York are represented in the formula. Depending on your knowledge of math, you can understand some of this, or little, or none. I first theorized that time could be traversed when doing my calculations writing the Philadelphia Experiment, in which I rigged a ship with special electrical apparatus and constituted a border around it with simple wire and electrodes similar to the screen. The ship was placed at a strategic point in the strange magnetic field of the Bermuda Triangle, and when the electric charge was applied, it traversed exactly fifteen minutes ahead in time. To the astonishment of the US Naval officers present on the other ship viewing it, it disappeared for fifteen minutes and then reappeared. The math involved in the screen you see is similar to the math I used for the Philadelphia Experiment. You could say this:

"The Manhattan Project was monumental, and the Philadelphia Experiment mystified them, but the Pittsburgh Experiment was a complete failure!"

The image on-screen suddenly showed Einstein at full body length in white laboratory coat stumbling and covering his eyes as two bombs exploded in the background. Then his face came back on-screen, showing him smiling and laughing.

"Ha-ha-ha. That was a joke. Well, I am not too good at making up jokes. Of course, there was no Pittsburgh Experiment. Anyway, I have some important things to tell you. Although you are only one man, to me you represent the whole public—the public of the future. Well, where do I begin. I was born in Ulm, Germany, on March 14, 1879. At one, my father moved our family to Munich and started an electrical shop. My earliest memories are of watching clocks being repaired in my father's shop. At first I did not show 'outgoingness' nor academic prodigy. My parents had no hope that I was gifted as a child. At twelve, I discovered a calculus book and began studying it. I could understand it clearly, and my comprehension of math began to culminate.

"I graduated from the Federal Polytechnic Academy in Zurich in 1900, became a Swiss citizen, worked for two months as a math teacher, then took a job at the Swiss patent office in Bern. In 1905, I published in the prestigious German physics monthly *Annalen der Physik* a thesis, 'A New Determination of Molecular Dimensions,' and it earned me a PhD from the University of Zurich. I wrote my most famous work in the form of four more papers appearing in Annalen. These essays advanced math and physical theory and changed man's scientific view of the universe, if I do say so myself. The first was 'On the Motion-Required by the Molecular Kinetic Theory of Heat of Small Particles Suspended in a Stationary Liquid.' The second was 'On a Heuristic Viewpoint Concerning the Production and Transformation of Light,' in which I explained the emission of electrons from some solids when struck by light and called it the photoelectric effect. The third essay was 'On the Electrodynamics of Moving Bodies.' It contained my special theory of relativity: if the speed of light is constant, both time and motion are relative to the observer. The fourth paper "Does the Inertia of a Body Depend upon Its Energy Content?" had in it my famous equation, energy equals mass times the speed of light squared, $E=mc^2$.

"In 1914, my wife was unable to return to where I lived then, Berlin, after she and my two sons had vacationed in Switzerland, with the eruption of World War I. A few years later, our separation became a divorce. They began to hail me as a great genius, some saying that I was the greatest genius on earth in 1919 after a scientific expedition to Principe Island in the Gulf of Guinea photographed a solar eclipse on May 29 and confirmed calculations made in my general theory of relativity, which concerned the slight bending of light in the gravitational field of the sun. After World War II, I enjoyed world fame and a place among the great minds of the scientific community. In the year 1930, my son Edward suffered mental breakdown. It was one of the low points of my life to see him that way. The coming of war and the Nazi regime, I knew threatened Germany and the rest of the world. I abhorred the war. Hitler was a madman. I had to flee Germany, being a Jew, in October 1933 after Hitler became chancellor. My favorite summer retreat lake house at Caputh, near Berlin, was ransacked by Nazi storm troopers. I agreed with Sigmund Freud that people have an innate lust for hatred and destruction. War, we agreed, is biologically sound because of the love-hate instincts of man.

"From then on, I made Princeton my home. I wrote to Roosevelt concerning the possibility of a super bomb, and the Manhattan Project was initiated, resulting in the calamities in Japan. Although it ended the war, I felt dropping the bomb was a grave mistake, which opened the door to a new era in warfare in which ultimate mass destruction would always be a lurking, ominous possibility. I decided to involve the rest of my life in the effort to create social awareness worldwide to never allow the use of the bomb. So far, we have done well.

"In 1949, the *New York Times* in a survey proclaimed that I, Albert Einstein, was the most popular man in the world. The news came to me in the evening when there were a few people in the house. I excused myself from the living room and walked into the bathroom. I stared at myself in the mirror for a long moment of self-discovery. It seemed that my whole life had culminated at this pinnacle, to be voted the number one most popular man on earth. I then jump-started and blurted out…'I don't care!'

"I shifted on my feet and then contorted, waving my arms. I broke out in a silly, ridiculous dance and started making up a rhyme as I lifted

my legs, twisted at the torso, and clapped my hands. I remember it going
something like this…

> So I'm the most popular scientist in the world
> Yes the mystery my friends has unfurled
> They say that I am genius number one
> And a nuclear era has begun
> But I don't care!
>
> The Nazi took over and created hate
> Germany was cast into war, and such was fate
> The allies bombed Germany all to hell
> The war was won and nothing left to tell
> But I don't care!
>
> The theory is that E equals mc squared
> And who thought this? 'Twas I who dared
> They rant and rave 'bout the theories of Einstein
> It's all molecular and relative, and I ain't lyin'
> But I don't care!
>
> They wouldn't let me on the Manhattan Project
> No security clearance, oh, well, what the heck
> They split the atom, now they have the bomb
> But don't blame me, folks, I ain't your mom
> And I don't care!
>
> A schmeckel is a schmeckel
> And a Jew is a Jew
> They say there's sometimes not much difference
> In between the two
>
> So clap your hands, jump up and down
> And hop and skip and prance
> I'll show you time and energy
> And the atomic Einstein dance!

Sha shoushka shoush and back and forth
I got ants in my pants
Left and right and eins, zwei, drei
You're doing the Einstein dance!

Yavolt, yavolt, and back and forth
Spin 'round and clap your hands
Up and down and round and round
You're doing the Einstein dance!

One, two, three, hey, look at me
Come on, and take a chance
In and out and plant your foot
You're doing the Einstein dance!

You're doing the Einstein dance!
You're doing the Einstein dance!
Kaput, kaput, and mazeltov
You're doing the Einstein dance!"

The image of Einstein dancing ridiculously on screen came to a halt. He sat back down to where it was only his face on screen, staring back at the man behind the desk.

He said, "In conclusion, I would like to say to you, whoever you are, I hope things are going well in your time. Let there never be a nuclear war! Amen. I hope that in your time, I am remembered for aspects of technology that have come of age applying my mathematics other than nuclear bombs. Good things. I'm sure that there are many inventions new to the world, making it a better place to live in. I did my part, and the torch is carried on. Peace and God's good will to you and all the future inhabitants of earth.

—Auf Wiedersehen."

About the Author

Reggie David has lived in many places in the US and had many jobs, including food industry work, construction work, and years doing Bering Sea commercial fishing. He spent years in Hawaii surfing, and he is an advanced surfer able to surf big waves. He attended the University of Maryland in the '90s.

Petrification is a collection of seventeen short stories. Beelzebub the demon has transported over time zones to arrive at the Rothchild's party to cause mayhem in "Now Meet Beelzebub the Hero." "The Subliminal Voice of Liberty" is a poem recited by a man in Shanty Town, Jamaica. "Morbidity" is a bizarre account of a person stuck in a cycle of hallucinating. "The Afterlife" describes different afterlife sequences for certain types of people. "When They *Les Miserables*" is a campy short about two police officers on the prowl to find vagrants and abuse them. "White Wedding" is a freak wedding completely disrupted. "Worse Than Kitsch" is a short, fat, bald guy narrating a typical day in advertising. "Petrification" is a sci-fi short about a man contracting a strange desert virus and becoming bodily dead but having brain activity continue in his mind for a month. "The Edge" is a solitary wild man existing on a tropical island alone. "360°" is a freakish rotation of an entire basketball arena during a game. "Unnamed" is an abstract entity that communicates telepathically with people and imitates a radio show. "The Beelzebub Interview" takes a freelance writer through history explaining catastrophic events and how they happened. And finally, Albert Einstein speaks to a man in the future through a special 'time warp screen' in "Einstein's Address to the Public of the Future".